## Verna m

## “Don’t touch me, Ward!”

She couldn’t bear the sweet agony of his caress. “You can forget your jungle madness,” she added. “This is civilization.”

A grim smile appeared on his lips. “Little Miss Cool has returned, I see. Where’s that hot, passionate woman I discovered?”

“Left behind, I hope,” she snapped. “Let’s get one thing straight. Whatever happened was a mistake, a moment of madness, if you like. I’ll be friends because that’s what my father wants, but as for anything else, you can forget it.”

“I don’t believe you, Verna,” Ward said tightly. “But if that’s the way you want to play it, then carry on. You’ll be the loser.”

He turned and left, and Verna’s eyes filled with tears. She wanted to call him back. She wanted him—on whatever terms.

MARGARET MAYO
is also the author of these
*Harlequin Romances*

1980—DESTINY PARADISE
1996—SHADES OF AUTUMN
2028—PERILOUS WATERS
2051—LAND OF ICE AND FIRE
2086—RAINBOW MAGIC
2118—SEA GYPSY
2280—AFRAID TO LOVE
2327—STORMY AFFAIR
2360—VALLEY OF THE HAWK
2385—BURNING DESIRE
2439—A TASTE OF PARADISE
2474—DIVIDED LOYALTIES

# Dangerous Journey

Margaret Mayo

Harlequin Books

TORONTO • NEW YORK • LOS ANGELES • LONDON
AMSTERDAM • PARIS • SYDNEY • HAMBURG
STOCKHOLM • ATHENS • TOKYO • MILAN

Original hardcover edition published in 1982
by Mills & Boon Limited

ISBN 0-373-02557-2

Harlequin Romance first edition July 1983



Printed in U.S.A.

# CHAPTER ONE

THE doorbell rang and Verna dragged herself impatiently out of bed. Jenny had forgotten her key again!

'One of these days——' she began as she opened the door, then stopped in a moment of panic at the sight of a stranger—a tall, dark, handsome man who looked at her with intense curiosity, and something else she could not quite fathom out.

She was so used to letting in her flatmate that it had not occurred to her to make sure. Quickly she slammed the door, but he was faster, his foot effectively stopped it from closing. 'Miss Verna Pemberton?' he enquired pleasantly.

Surprised that he should know her name, Verna momentarily released her grip. Taking advantage, he swung the door wide, his immense frame filling the doorway. 'Aren't you going to ask me in?'

His easy smile, revealing perfectly even white teeth, was calculated to charm, but Verna was too suspicious to be impressed. 'Who are you, and what do you want?'

'My name's Levitt,' he said, 'Ward Levitt, and I'm a friend of your father.'

She looked at him sharply. 'Try again, Mr Levitt—my father's dead.'

Keen blue eyes insolently scanned her body in its short cotton nightdress. He grinned wryly. 'I need to talk to you—maybe we should shut the door. Anyone seeing you like that might get the wrong idea.'

Verna's head jerked. For one moment she had

forgotten what she was wearing! Now she snatched up a coat that lay on the back of the settee, holding it in front of her like a shield.

'You choose a strange time to come calling, Mr Levitt.' Her green eyes flashed angrily. 'I'd prefer it if you went.'

'I only arrived in England today,' he said. 'I came straight here. I thought maybe you could put me up for the night?'

'Then you'd best think again,' she countered hostilely. 'Even if I knew you, I wouldn't allow you to stay.'

'Admirable principles,' he nodded. 'Your father will be proud of you.'

'My father died when I was a baby,' she said coldly, impatiently. 'I don't know who you are or why you're here, but will you please go!'

He shrugged easily. 'Where's the nearest hotel? And for your sake I hope they have rooms, or you'll find me back here double quick.'

'Round the corner,' she returned tightly, 'and the next time I shall be prepared. The door will remain firmly closed.'

'Not when you hear what I have to say,' came his enigmatic reply. '*Adeus*, sweet lady. I'll see you tomorrow.'

When he had gone Verna sank limply down on to the settee, completely bewildered. What had all that been about? Who was Ward Levitt? What did he want? Maybe she ought to have invited him in after all. He had certainly aroused her curiosity.

She was still sitting when Jenny returned. The girl took one look at her friend. 'What's the matter with you? I thought you were having an early night?'

'I had a visitor,' Verna explained. 'A man who claims to know my father.'

Jenny frowned. 'But didn't he die when——'

'That's right,' nodded Verna. 'That's the puzzling part. I wonder what he really wanted?'

'It's unlike you not to find out,' said Jenny. 'Why did you send him away without satisfying your curiosity?'

'Because I was dressed like this,' cried Verna. 'I thought it was you forgotten your key again. Heavens, I'd have never opened the door if I'd known! At least I can be thankful he didn't force his way in, though the way he looked at me I'm surprised.'

'An honourable man,' mocked Jenny. 'Was he good-looking too?'

'Not so honourable,' replied Verna. 'He said he'd only just arrived in England and he wanted to stay here. Can you imagine it? My God, I won't even let David do that, and look how long I've known him!'

'Dear dependable David,' laughed Jenny. 'He wouldn't harm a fly. But tell me more about this intriguing stranger who caught you in your nightie.'

Verna smiled ruefully. 'Actually, he was fantastically good-looking. You know, the sort you dream about—tall, dark, rugged, bronzed, with the most intense blue eyes I've ever seen.'

'And you turned him away!' chided her friend. 'I wish I'd been here.'

'He's coming back tomorrow,' said Verna. 'Hang around, you can see him then. Actually I'd be glad of your moral support.'

'I don't believe it!' Jenny raised her brows in mock surprise. 'Verna Pemberton afraid of a man? I thought you knew how to handle the opposite sex. Don't tell me you've met your match!'

Verna picked up a cushion and threw it at Jenny.

'Wait till you see him, you'll know exactly what I mean.'

For a long time that night Verna lay awake, pondering over her mysterious visitor, unable to even hazard a guess at what he might want. He claimed to know her father—yet her mother had told her that he was dead, and she knew who she would rather believe.

Quite clearly it was a tale he had invented to get to know her, but why? And how had he found out her name and where she lived? And where had he come from?

She was up early the next morning and on tenterhooks each time the doorbell rang. The girls had many friends and it was as though they all decided to visit them. By lunchtime Verna's nerves were definitely ragged, and she decided to go for a walk.

'I can't stand it any longer,' she said to Jenny. 'If *he* comes, take a message, find out what he wants, and then get rid of him.'

Jenny grinned. 'Getting under your skin, is he? He must certainly be some man. I've never seen you like this before. You're usually so cool and calm.'

Verna tossed her blonde hair angrily. 'I'm annoyed because he said he was coming and he hasn't. I do think people should keep to their word.'

'Did he give any time?' asked Jenny reasonably.

'Actually, no,' admitted Verna. 'But if it was important enough for him to come here at half past ten last night why the hell didn't he come round early this morning?'

Even as she spoke the bell went again. Verna felt a prickle of alarm run down her spine. 'That's him,' she said. 'You answer the door. The way I feel at this very second I'll slam it in his face!'

'And then you'll never find out what he wants,' chuckled Jenny. 'Sit down and collect yourself, Verna—I don't want a free fight on my hands!'

The girls' flat was on the ground floor of a large house, their living room opening directly into the communal hall outside. Ward Levitt leaned indolently against the door frame, and turned his charming smile upon Jenny as she opened the door. Behind him was a girl from the flat above, staring with open curiosity at the handsome stranger.

'You'd better come in,' said Jenny quickly, recognising him immediately from Verna's description. 'We have some mighty inquisitive neighbours around here.'

The girl moved on, but not before she had given the dark-haired man another interested and admiring glance.

He entered the room and Jenny closed the door behind him. Verna drew a deep breath and looked up. He seemed even taller than she remembered, filling the room with his breadth and height, and there was something else about him, too, a certain magnetism that drew her eyes to him whether she liked it or not.

He held out his hand. 'Good morning, Miss Pemberton. I trust you slept well?'

She stood up, but ignored his hand, crossing towards the window and pretending to look out at the expanse of lawn. 'Not really,' she said tightly. 'Suppose you tell me why you're here?'

Jenny said, 'Would you like a cup of tea, Mr—er—Levitt?'

Verna spun, in time to see her friend bestow a warm smile upon their visitor. 'No!' she said sharply. 'Mr Levitt will not be staying that long.'

He grinned. 'In other words, dear lady, Miss Pemberton doesn't trust herself alone with me.

Why don't you both make the tea? I'll sit and wait. It's been a long time since I had a good cup of English tea.'

He suited his words by lowering himself lazily into one of their armchairs, looking very much at home, and quite oblivious to Verna's angry expression.

Jenny took her hand and pulled her into the kitchen. 'Wow,' she exclaimed, 'he's some dish! If you don't want him, I'll have him.'

'You're welcome,' replied Verna crossly. 'The more I see of him the more I dislike him. He's too smooth, too charming. He's up to something, and I wish I knew what.'

'You're hardly giving yourself chance to find out,' said Jenny, filling the kettle and plugging it in.

'It's strange,' insisted Verna, setting cups and saucers on to a tray, 'his turning up here like this. I don't trust him.'

'But you're curious all the same?' queried her friend.

Verna shrugged. 'I suppose so, who wouldn't be? But I wish he'd come to the point instead of keeping me in suspense.'

'And whose fault is that?' laughed Jenny. 'You're ready to declare war instead of listening to what he has to say.'

'Because I know it will be all lies.'

Jenny shook her head impatiently. 'He'd hardly be here if he hadn't some genuine reason. What's wrong with you, Verna?'

'I don't know.' Verna sat down at the table and rested her head glumly on her hands.

'I do,' said Jenny. 'You're used to being in control. You run all the men in your life, you always have, and because here's one man who's obviously got the upper hand you don't like it.'

Reluctantly Verna had to admit that this was true. Her mother had drummed it into her as a girl that men were only ever after one thing, and for this reason Verna had always kept them at arm's length, mastering them in her own sweet way so that they never realised what she was doing.

They never lasted long. Only David had been around for more time than she could remember. David, the artist, who saw her only as a form of art, an object to paint—a beautiful woman, but not one whom he desired as a man normally desires a woman. And this suited Verna. Their relationship was perfect so far as she was concerned.

But Ward Levitt! Here was a man she could never hope to dominate, and in some inexplicable way he posed a threat. He disturbed her, and although she was curious as to why he was here she was also strangely afraid. And this was possibly the reason why she did not wish to hear what he had to say.

Jenny made the tea, but before carrying the tray through to the living room she said to her friend, 'Are you sure you want me in with you? I mean, it may be something very private that this man has to discuss.'

'I hardly think so,' said Verna. 'In any case, you're my friend. I have no secrets from you—and this is the first time I've ever felt the need for moral support. Don't let me down.'

He rose as they entered, taking the tray from Jenny and placing it carefully on the table. 'I don't think I caught your name,' he said, showing the white flash of his teeth against deep mahogany skin.

Jenny succumbed instantly. 'Jenny,' she said shyly.

'And you share this flat with Verna? Are rooms

like this much sought after? If your friend left would you soon find someone to take her place?'

'What are you talking about?' snapped Verna. 'I have no intention of going. I'm quite happy here, thank you very much.'

He smiled easily and resumed his seat. 'I've no doubt you are, but life doesn't stand still. There's always change.'

'If you've come to throw me out of this flat——' began Verna angrily.

He held up his hand. 'Please, don't get on your high horse. This place is nothing to do with me. I was merely generalising.'

Verna tossed her head, eyeing him scornfully. 'Suppose you tell me exactly why you're here, Mr Levitt?'

'A cup of tea first, I think,' he said, 'and then we'll get down to business. Ah, thank you, Jenny.'

He sipped his tea with annoying slowness until Verna felt like throwing her cup at him. She eyed him rebelliously, noting the long, lean length of him, the expensive mohair suit which sat perfectly on his broad shoulders. He was in complete control of the situation—and enjoying every minute of it, fully aware of her edginess but doing precious little to alleviate it.

Finally he passed his empty cup to Jenny. 'Thank you, Jenny-Wren, that was very nice.' He gave her one of his smiles and Verna guessed by Jenny's expression that her friend was totally overcome by this man's charm.

She strummed her fingers on the arms of her chair.

'I see patience is not one of your virtues,' remarked Ward Levitt, his eyes amused. 'Before I tell you why I'm here first of all let me confirm that you're Verna Pemberton and that your mother was Pamela Walton before she married?'

Verna nodded. 'That's right—but what's it got to do with you?'

'Your father sent me to find you,' he announced calmly.

'My father is dead,' repeated Verna tiredly. 'Don't start on that again!'

He inclined his head gravely. 'Your mother led you to believe that. In point of fact she left him when you were a mere six months old.'

'I don't believe you!' cried Verna hotly.

'Why should I make it up?' he asked logically. He put his hand into his breast pocket and pulled out a photograph. 'This is your father. There's no mistaking your relationship.'

Suspiciously Verna took it, and her heart jerked in a strange way as she gazed at the face. They both had the same determined chin, that was for sure, and his eyes were remarkably like her own. But her nose was pert and turned up like her mother's, nothing like the aristocratic lines of the man staring out at her from the picture. She thrust it back. 'You could have picked any one of a dozen girls. Why should I believe you?'

'Because it would make an old man happy.'

He sounded sincere, but Verna found it difficult to believe him. 'If what you say is true,' she probed, 'why did my mother leave him? Why did she make up a lie about him being dead?'

He looked at her sadly. 'You lost your mother twelve months ago in a road accident, is that right?'

She nodded, frowning. It frightened her that he knew so much.

'I feel, therefore, that I can speak of her without you judging me too harshly. Your father was a great deal older than Pamela, and he was very rich.'

'Are you suggesting she married him for his money?' broke in Verna wildly. 'What a despicable thing to say! My mother wasn't like that. She had money of her own. What would she want his for?'

He smiled wryly. 'Any money your mother had came from Guy Pemberton. He gave her a generous allowance. Despite the fact that she ran out on him he still loved her. He's some fellow, your father, and it would make him very happy if you went to live with him now.'

Verna was silent for several long minutes, digesting the information Ward Levitt had just fed her. It sounded highly suspect, yet why should he make up such a story? What could he possibly hope to gain? 'Why hasn't my father, supposing your story is true, got in touch with me before?' she queried roughly.

'He's been trying to find you,' he explained patiently. 'Ever since he had news of your mother's death.'

'He kept in touch?'

He shook his head. 'The allowance was cabled through to her bank, each year. It was the bank who informed Guy of Pamela's accident. Ever since then he's been like a man demented trying to trace you. Why did you leave your home without a forwarding address?'

'Memories,' she said simply. 'I'd always fancied London, but when Mum was alive I would never have dreamt of leaving her. Who are you, a private investigator?'

His brows rose. 'Do I look like one? No, he's tried that, with no result. I think I was his last resort. I was coming to England, so I said I'd do what I could to trace you.'

'And how come you've succeeded when trained

men haven't?' asked Verna scathingly. 'If you ask me, you're spinning some tale for reasons known only to yourself. I'd be pleased if you'd go, Mr Levitt. I'm in no mood for sick jokes like this.'

Jenny touched her friend's arm. 'I know this has nothing to do with me and I shouldn't interfere, but he sounds genuine. Why don't you give him the benefit of the doubt? You've got nothing to lose by going to see whether this man really is your father.'

Verna said savagely, 'He still hasn't told me how he found me. No, I think he's up to something. He's probably got a whole list of names. What are you, Mr Levitt, a night club owner touting for new hostesses?' Her green eyes were icily contemptuous. 'Just cross me off, will you? I'm afraid I don't play those sort of games.'

A flash of anger crossed his face, but the next moment he had himself under perfect control. 'Jenny-Wren,' he said persuasively, 'you seem a reasonable girl, can you please assure your friend that I have no ulterior motives, that I'm here strictly to help my friend Guy Pemberton find his daughter? What proof does she want? How can I convince her that I'm legitimate?'

'How did you know where I lived?' asked Verna heatedly.

'By a very strange coincidence,' he admitted. 'I was in touch with a colleague a week or two ago and I mentioned that while I was over here I intended to look for you. Not that I thought you'd be in London—I'd planned to start my search in your home town. He took your name, said he would help if he could, then suddenly came up with the astonishing news that a Verna Pemberton worked for a friend of his. It was such an unusual name that he was convinced you must be one and the same. I did some checking, and I too was ninety nine per cent sure that you were Guy's daughter.'

'And you told him this before you came over here? Is he expecting you to take me back with you to—wherever it is you live?'

'Brazil,' he said shortly. 'No, I didn't want to raise his hopes—in case you weren't the right person. But now I have no doubts. You are Guy's daughter, there's no getting away from it. The resemblance is striking.'

Verna suddenly did not know what to say. His story was plausible. But Brazil?

Silently he handed her the photograph 'I realise this must be a great shock. Perhaps you'd like time to think it over? I shall be pretty tied up this week, but I'll call again next weekend.'

He had left the flat before either of the girls could say anything. The silence between them lengthened until Jenny finally said, 'How about that? A rich daddy, eh? Aren't you excited?'

Verna shook her head. 'Maybe he is my father, maybe he isn't. But to me he'd be a stranger, and I don't see any point in meeting him. We would have nothing at all in common. I know nothing about him and he knows nothing about me. Any girl could go and say she was me. You could. How would he know the difference?'

'You'd feel the tie,' said Jenny. 'You know what they say about blood being thicker than water. I think you ought to go. Brazil! It sounds exciting. I mean, if you don't hit it off you can always come back, and you'll have had a holiday into the bargain.'

'I don't know.' Verna was not totally convinced. 'It's tempting, I must admit, but I still can't see why my mother lied. Do you think he's genuine? Or do you think I'd be putting my head into some sort of noose if I went along with him?'

'He's genuine,' said Jenny confidently. 'He's no con man—I'd put my life in his hands any day.'

Verna had to smile. 'You always were a sucker for a handsome face.'

For the rest of that week Verna was in a quandary. She found it difficult to concentrate on her work and constantly she looked at the photograph of Guy Pemberton, until finally she became convinced that he really was her father.

It was strange looking at a mirror image of her own eyes and she could not help wondering why he had never tried to see her. It hurt also that her mother should have kept this secret all these years.

Why was it? she wondered. Had she been afraid that she would lose her daughter? That if Verna knew she had a father she would want to go to him and maybe prefer to live with him rather than Pamela?

Gradually the urge to see him grew stronger—until finally she knew that when Ward Levitt returned at the weekend she would agree to go back with him to Brazil.

She found herself waiting for his visit with an eagerness that was unlike her usual self, and her heartbeats quickened each time the doorbell rang. This could be the beginning of a new era in her life, maybe a new life in Brazil! It was a country she knew nothing about, and this unexpected trip posed all sorts of exciting possibilities.

When Ward Levitt eventually arrived it was late Sunday evening. Verna had given him up, saying to Jenny that she had been right all along and he was no more genuine than she had supposed.

His wide smile embraced the two girls and Jenny, all of a dither, disappeared into the kitchen to make a pot of tea.

He sat down without being asked, sinking into one of the deep armchairs, stretching his long legs out in front of him, completely relaxed.

'Do make yourself at home.' An edge of annoyance sounded in Verna's voice.

'You look uneasy,' he said, studying her closely. 'Is anything wrong? Are you still having difficulty in making up your mind?'

She lifted her fine brows. 'None at all, Mr Levitt,' she said coldly.

'Good, then you're coming? Guy will be pleased. Actually I phoned him and told him the good news, and he's so excited you won't believe it.'

His confidence irritated her beyond reason. 'Wasn't that rather jumping the gun? As a matter of fact I'm not coming. I've decided it's too big a risk to take on the offchance that this man might, just might, be my father. If he's that keen to find me he can come here.'

He frowned and his fingers gripped the arm of the chair. Long fingers, she noted inconsequentially, well manicured. Capable hands, powerful hands, hands that could inflict physical punishment should he so choose.

Now, why was she thinking along those lines? He had not threatened her. Yet somehow he presented a picture of strength, of always being in command of any situation, not too happy when his plans were thwarted, prepared to take whatever action he thought necessary to get his own way.

She waited with bated breath for his reply.

'Guy's not well enough to make the journey,' he said quietly, but although his tones were low they were intimidating, telling her more surely than any words that he considered she was making a mistake, that it was her duty to go to this man who claimed to be her father.

Her eyes met his and held, and the intense blueness pierced through her, giving the impression that he was able to see right into her mind.

It was unnerving to say the least, but she was determined not to be put on by Ward Levitt. Up until this point she had remained standing; now she took the seat opposite him, still without her eyes leaving his face. 'Then that's his bad luck,' she said coldly. 'I'm very happy here, why should I throw it all away on the whim of some old man?'

His lips thinned and a pulse jerked in his jaw. 'Guy is a very good friend and neighbour of mine, and I can assure you it's no whim. He's done everything in his power to trace you, and I'm goddamn sure that you're not going to slip through my fingers now.'

Verna smiled, finding this verbal battle somehow exhilarating. She was a fiercely independent girl, full of self-confidence, and usually in complete control of any situation. It was a change for her to meet someone who was ready to do battle, who did not submit to her somewhat forceful personality.

Ward Levitt was a challenge.

'And what do you propose to do—carry me there under your arm?'

He did not return her smile. 'Somehow, I don't think that will be necessary. I think you're bluffing, Miss Pemberton. I think that you've said no merely to test my reaction.'

He was right, curse him! But she said, 'How wrong you are, Mr Levitt. Surely if you've done your homework correctly you'll realise that I have a very responsible job that I'm not likely to give up at the drop of a hat.'

'Mr Johnson can find another buyer.'

She frowned. 'You know him?'

'I made it my duty to introduce myself,' he said calmly. 'I needed to make sure you were the right person before I contacted you. He was very helpful. He said he'll be sorry to lose you but he realises that family ties came first.'

Verna was furious. 'How dare you! *How dare you*, Mr Levitt! Please go, before I lose my temper altogether and start throwing things!'

He smiled crookedly. 'Somehow I don't think it will come to that—you're far too sensible. Think about it rationally. There's a man in Brazil eating his heart out for you—he's your father, your flesh and blood. Could you ever forgive yourself if you didn't go to him? Wouldn't it be for ever on your mind that there could be a weary old man willing to love you, to share his home, to shower you with gifts—to take you into his heart?'

But Verna was far from moved. 'What a marvellous ambassador he has in you,' she scoffed. 'How much farther are you prepared to go to make me change my mind?'

He shook his head. 'You might look like Guy, but you certainly don't get your temperament from him. Is that your mother coming out in you?'

Her eyes flashed angrily. 'My mother was a very wonderful person. She brought me up single-handed. She taught me to be independent—and extremely wary of men like you!'

He looked amused. 'My guess is that you've not met many men like me. I should imagine that you twist most of them round your little finger. They're either fascinated or frightened by you. Myself, I prefer a woman a little more feminine. I don't like dominant females.'

Without stopping to think Verna picked up an ash tray and threw it. It went a mile off its target, falling harmlessly to the floor, and seemed to amuse Ward Levitt even more. 'Tut, tut,' he chided. 'You really ought to learn to control that temper, it could get you into trouble.'

She glared, but took refuge in silence, and Jenny chose that moment to enter with the tray of tea. She smiled at their visitor. 'Sorry I've been so long, but I thought you'd have plenty to discuss. Isn't it wonderful Verna agreeing to fly out with you to see her father? She's hardly talked of anything else these last few days.'

Verna could have hit her! A slow smile spread over Ward Levitt's face. 'It's fantastic news, Jenny-Wren. The best thing I've heard in a long time.'

## CHAPTER TWO

VERNA had spent a hectic few days shopping for lightweight clothes, having the necessary injections for South America, and reading up all she could on Brazil. It did not sound a particularly enticing sort of place, full of insects and all sorts of unpleasant things.

Now they were preparing to land at Rio. The twelve-hour flight had been a nightmare. She was excited at the thought of meeting Guy Pemberton, but being compelled to travel with the obnoxious Ward Levitt took away most of her pleasure. And he too made no secret of the fact that he was not exactly enthralled at having her as a travelling companion, for the most part burying his nose in a book. She kept remembering his statement that she was not his type. Someone more feminine! This really caught Verna on the raw.

She was not unattractive, she knew without being immodest, indeed she had never been short of admirers, and it niggled her to think that this man had had the gall to say that she was bossy.

Unconsciously she smoothed her blonde hair, pushed back the waves from her face, her chin held proudly erect. He glanced at her, as he had many times during the flight. 'Are you nervous? There's no need to be. Guy is the nicest, kindest person you could wish to meet.'

It was not the thought of her impending meeting that made her edgy, she could have told him. It was his offhand treatment, his attitude that he was only accompanying her as a favour to his friend, not because he was enjoying it.

The least he could have done was keep his feelings to himself, attempt to put her at her ease for what was the journey of a lifetime. He really was the most infuriating man she had ever met!

'I'm all right,' she said, staring pointedly out of the window. Rio was coming up to meet them, an enchanting city set in the midst of emerald green hills.

As the plane lost height she could see houses built into the hillsides, and above them the strange shanty communities, called *favellas*, which she had read about in her thirst for knowledge on Brazil.

But dominating everything was the statue of Christ perched high on the mountainside, arms outstretched in the attitude of the Crucifixion. Verna spoke spontaneously. 'Corcovado! Isn't it magnificent? I read about it the other day, but I never realised it would be quite so impressive. It's huge.'

Her companion smiled drily. 'It's quite something, I suppose. I've grown used to seeing it. It no longer intrigues me.'

'No, I shouldn't imagine it would,' she commented, some of her pleasure fading. 'You don't strike me as a man with aesthetic tastes.'

His brows rose. 'And on what do you base that supposition?'

She shrugged. 'Nothing in particular. It's just a feeling I have.'

'You must tell me more about these *feelings* one day,' he said. 'They could be interesting.'

The plane landed smoothly and in the space of a few minutes they were stepping from the cabin and down the steps on to the tarmac.

Verna was unprepared for the heat which met them. She had taken his advice and worn a lightweight trouser suit, but even so it felt decidedly too much against her skin in the thick humid heat which quite took her breath away.

Before she had reached the Customs shed perspiration trickled down her body, her clothes sticking uncomfortably, 'Phew!' she said to her companion. 'You never warned me about this.'

He grinned. 'I told you it would be hot.'

He, damn him, looked remarkably cool. 'But not sticky. I can't breathe. Is it always like this?'

'I can't say I've noticed,' he replied indifferently. 'You'll get used to it.'

It took an age to get through Customs, the officials were in no hurry, but finally they managed it and climbed into a waiting taxi which Verna presumed would take her to her father's house.

To her surprise it stopped in front of a hotel. She glared at the man beside her. 'What is this? Why have you brought me here? Where is—Guy Pemberton?'

He grinned easily. 'He lives in Belém. Tonight we stay here. Tomorrow we'll fly to your father.'

She eyed him suspiciously. 'I'm beginning to wonder whether there really is such a man as Guy Pemberton. I have the most horrible feeling that you've got me here under false pretences.'

'Do I look like a man who'd do that?' he asked, blue eyes wide and innocent.

'Yes, you do!' she snapped. 'Oh, come on, let's get inside. I can't stand this heat much longer.'

The cool blast of the air-conditioning hit them as they went into the foyer. It was so welcome that Verna forgot her annoyance, for a moment relaxing sufficiently to say, 'This is nice.'

'I'm glad something pleases you.'

His biting comment quickly needled her again. 'I don't think I'm that impossible,' she said heatedly.

'No?' The thick brows rose yet again. 'I would say you've been pretty well impossible from the moment we met, and I'm afraid Guy is going to have his hands more full than he realises.'

'It's you who's the difficult one,' she cried recklessly, before realising that they were causing a great deal of interest. She looked around selfconsciously, then hissed, 'Find out which are our rooms. I need a shower.'

The room was cool and shaded and it did not take Verna more than a few seconds to strip off her clothes.

Ward Levitt had warned her it would be hot in Brazil, but he had certainly given no indication that the heat would be so enervating. She could have been in it for no more than an hour, yet she felt as clammy as though she had been in a Turkish bath.

She stood for several minutes beneath the jets of water, then dressed in one of her new sleeveless cotton dresses. She felt better, not nearly so irritable, and when a tap came on her door she called, 'Come in,' quite cheerfully.

Ward Levitt looked even more handsome, if that was possible, in a crisp white shirt and cream trousers. The pale colours emphasised his tan and the rolled-back sleeves revealed muscular arms. His hair curled damply about his forehead and his blue eyes studied her with interest.

'You look better,' he said, 'I've asked for drinks to be sent up. I thought you might want to rest a while before exploring the city.'

Verna thought of the heat outside. 'Do we have to?' she asked. 'I don't think I could stand it.'

'You'll get acclimatised,' he said. 'And of course you must see Rio. Belém's over a thousand miles from here, and you might not get another chance.'

Verna was horrified. 'So far? I had no idea!'

'You're not in England now,' he laughed. 'You'll have to get used to much greater distances. Don't worry, I have my own plane, it won't take too long.'

It got worse by the second. She stared at him aghast. '*Your* plane? You mean you'll be flying it yourself? Just you and me?'

'I am qualified,' he returned irately. 'You have nothing to worry about.'

'Oh, I'm not worried,' she said airily. In fact she was terrified. She did not really like flying—even in a jet—but in some little private plane? It did not bear thinking about.

It was a relief when their drinks arrived and she could focus her attention on something else. He had ordered lager for himself, and for her a *pingo*, which he informed her was *cachaça*, a local spirit, mixed with ice and fresh lime juice. The taste was certainly different from anything else she had ever had, fiery and strong, but ice-cold and refreshing, and she felt a whole lot better for it.

'Are you hungry?' he asked. 'Do you want to eat? Or shall we do our sightseeing first and then eat later?'

'You don't have to show me Rio,' she said, gaining the impression that he was merely acting out of politeness, that he really had no interest in touring the city.

'Oh, I do,' he replied. 'It will be the first thing your father asks me.'

She looked at him questioningly. 'You care what he thinks? You amaze me. I wouldn't have thought you'd give two hoots for anyone else's opinion.'

'Guy Pemberton is one of the few people I do care about,' he said slowly. 'If it wasn't for him, I wouldn't be taking you anywhere.'

Verna clamped her lips. He certainly had a knack

of making her feel uncomfortable! 'Then don't bother,' she said sharply. 'I'll stay here until you're ready to leave.' At least it would be cooler. She took a further mouthful of her drink, choked over the unusual taste, and glared at him angrily.

He laughed. 'What a firecracker you are! At least there's no chance of being bored by your company. One never knows what you're going to say next.'

Her fingers tightened on the glass, and her green eyes were hostile.

He held up his hand. 'No, don't throw it,' he said. 'The management wouldn't take kindly to their glasses being smashed against the wall.'

'I wouldn't miss—not again,' she grated. 'But you could be right. I shall reserve the pleasure for some other time.'

His lips quirked. 'Never a dull moment! Finish your drink, and let's go, before I'm tempted to put you to the test.'

Silently fuming, she emptied her glass and slammed it down on the table. He hooked a hand through her arm as they left the hotel, but she snatched away. 'Don't touch me!' she snapped.

He tensed, but was not noticeably angry. 'Would Miss Pemberton prefer a tour of the shops, or perhaps a ride in the cable car up Sugar Loaf Mountain?' he enquired mockingly.

Verna thought of the heat, and the inevitable close proximity of this man in the cable car, and voted for the shops. They were sure to be air-conditioned and she would be able to wander at will—and hopefully lose him!

'Rio has the reputation in Latin America for being one of the best places to shop,' her companion told her. 'But you must be prepared to bargain. They inevitably start off with high prices.'

He was right. The articles for sale were wide and

varied, the clothes so rich in variety and superb in taste that they quite took Verna's breath away. She wanted to buy so much, but restricted herself to one exquisite dress in a high quality cotton, beautifully patterned in blues and greens, which brought out the colour in her eyes and was a vivid contrast against the paleness of her skin.

She wished she had had time to get an artificial tan before coming here. The Brazilian girls were all beautifully suntanned and perfectly groomed, and although she had felt fresh herself when first leaving the hotel, now she began to feel definitely jaded, her white skin soaked with perspiration until she felt as though she was going to melt.

Most of the shops were air-conditioned, as she had anticipated, but even this was not sufficient to counteract the heat outside.

Ward Levitt on the other hand continued to look cool and unflustered, ushering her from shop to shop with the utmost courtesy. There were beautiful leather shops and gem shops, but before long Verna lost interest. She had had more than she could stand.

'We'll find a café,' he decided, gazing with amusement at her shining, perspiration-beaded face. 'A long, cool drink is what you need.'

'And another shower,' she said sharply. 'Is it always like this?'

'You'll find Belém even more humid,' he warned. 'This is quite pleasant in comparison. And of course it's summer. Coming from England in January to this is a complete change. You'll adjust.'

Verna did not think so, but she shrugged, and said, 'I hope you're right. I feel as if I want to pass out!'

He looked at her sharply and took her arm, and this time she did not object. She did indeed feel decidedly wobbly at the knees. She was normally so fit and well that it irritated her to think that she had weakened, especially in front of this man.

Once sitting, in a spacious room where blasts of cold air kept the place delightfully cool, Verna began to feel better. She drank gratefully the cold Coca-Cola Ward placed before her, asking for another as soon as the first was finished.

'I think I'd like to go back to the hotel,' she said at length, 'and lie down for a while.'

He nodded, surprisingly agreeable, and looked at his watch. 'Good idea. We have a couple of hours before dinner. I could do with a rest myself.'

Somehow this did not quite ring true. Perhaps he was humouring her? Though that did not seem like him either. But she was too tired to question him, and let her lethargy fall over her like a cloak.

They took a taxi and passed a crowded beach where bronzed Brazilians lay on straw mats beneath striped umbrellas, their near-naked bodies gleaming with oil. White skyscrapers shimmered in the heat, mountains rose sharply round the city, the unforgettable figure of Christ crowning the highest.

It was a beautiful, magical place, but Verna wished the heat was not quite so overpowering. Perhaps, as Ward said, she would get used to it. She hoped so, otherwise she could not see herself remaining in Brazil for very long.

The English weather might not be the best in the world, but at this moment she decided it was infinitely preferable.

After yet another shower, she lay down on the bed completely naked and fell asleep instantly, waking when a sharp tap came on the door and Ward called that it was almost time for dinner.

Afraid he might come in, she said sharply that

she would be no more than five minutes, and scrambled into yet another clean dress. At this rate she would use up all her clothes before she got to her destination!

Their meal was delicious—shrimps in a rich hot, tomato-type sauce, boiled duck with rice and more tomatoes, a mixed salad, all washed down with a light, well-chilled Brazilian wine. Coffee came in tiny cups, very sweet, thick and black, which Ward told her the Brazilians drank copiously. It was not to her liking, but she finished it from sheer politeness, refusing, however, a second cup.

'What time are we leaving?' she asked.

He shrugged and smiled. 'Have you not heard of Brazilian time? Who knows? I asked for the plane to be ready by nine, but it could be anything up to three hours late. No one hurries here.'

What have I let myself in for? wondered Verna. 'I see,' she said. 'And how long do you reckon it will take us to get to Belém?'

'Twelve hours, including a stop for refuelling.'

He said it as though it was nothing, but Verna was horrified. It had taken them that length of time from London to Rio, she had never imagined that another equally long journey awaited her at this end.

'Twelve hours?' she repeated incredulously, wondering how she would ever get through it cooped in a tiny cabin with this man. It would be different if it was with someone she liked—or who liked her! But Ward Levitt? It would be sheer purgatory.

'Does it bother you?' he asked drily, eyes narrowed so that she was unable to read their expression.

'Not in the slightest,' she lied, chin tilted, looking straight into his face.

He smiled wryly. 'Little liar. It bothers you one heck of a lot. What is it, don't you trust me? Don't worry, I shall have my hands full flying the plane. You'll be quite safe.'

'The thought never crossed my mind,' she returned tightly. 'It's the plane that worries me. Is that safe?'

'I sure as hell hope so,' he laughed. 'It's done me faithful service up till now. I have no reason to doubt its capabilities.'

When their meal was finished Ward seemed in no hurry to move from their table, smoking small cheroots one after the other, sometimes looking at her through the thin haze of smoke, at others leaning back in his chair and gazing into space.

Verna wondered what he was thinking.

'About Guy,' he said suddenly. 'Have you really accepted that he's your father? It would upset him greatly if you turned up and then rejected him.'

Verna's eyes sparked. 'Then you shouldn't have raised his hopes. If anything goes wrong it will be your fault.' She glared at the man opposite, her antagonism so strong that she felt like walking out—except that she had nowhere to go!

'I don't think so. I'm already convinced, I was merely wondering how you felt. You've not once mentioned him. I would have thought a girl in your position would ply me with questions about a man she's just discovered is the father she thought dead.'

'I prefer to wait and judge for myself,' she replied coolly. 'In theory I accept that it could conceivably be him, but I think that until we meet neither of us can be sure. It puzzles me why my mother lied. Why would she want to deny me my father? It doesn't make sense.'

'It does,' he said. 'Your father fought tooth and

nail to get custody of you—but the law was on your mother's side. She swore, when she won the case, that she would never let him see his daughter again, and even though it was decreed he could have reasonable access, he was so hurt by Pamela's attitude that he gave up. He left England, made a life for himself out here. His love for your mother was a very rare kind—it was a pity she was the bitch she was.' These last words were said angrily, causing Verna to flare up with annoyance.

'How dare you call my mother names! You're in no position to condemn, Mr Levitt. It has nothing at all to do with you.'

His fingers strummed on the table top. 'On the contrary, Guy has confided in me all his fears—and desires. I worked for him, at one time I lived with him, now I have a place of my own, we're neighbours, and the best of friends. I know as much about Guy as he does himself.'

'I can't see that you're much of a friend if you talk about my mother like that,' she snapped. 'You're despicable, Mr Levitt, and I may as well tell you now that I'm not looking forward to the journey with you tomorrow, not one little bit. The thought of being in your company for twelve hours makes me sick!'

'I'm not exactly enamoured with the situation myself,' he returned swiftly. 'I had hoped that Guy's daughter would be a person he could be proud of, not someone as coldly unfeeling as you.'

Verna frowned ferociously. 'You certainly don't believe in pulling punches, do you, Mr Levitt?'

'I believe in being honest,' he replied calmly. 'I really thought you'd be overjoyed, not as unmoved as you make out.'

She shrugged. 'It's difficult for me to accept. Perhaps when I meet this Guy fellow I'll feel differently, but until then I prefer to reserve judgment.'

'And if you don't accept him, how do you think he'll feel?'

'I can't see that it will have anything to do with me,' she said coolly. 'If I have the slightest doubt that he's not my father then I shall catch the next plane home again. You'd do well to bear that in mind. I really do hope you haven't raised his hopes too much. You might be making a terrible mistake.'

'I don't think so.' His keen eyes watched her closely. 'There's too much of Guy in you for me to be mistaken.' There was a quirk to his lips as he spoke.

Verna said sharply, 'What do you mean?'

'Mannerisms, expressions—but certainly not your temper. He's one of the most placid men I've ever met.'

'It's a wonder my mother ever left this—paragon of virtue,' she returned drily.

'She had her own reasons, I expect,' he shrugged. 'It's the one thing Guy never discusses.'

'Maybe it was his fault, then,' she snapped. 'If you'll excuse me, I think I'll go to bed. I must prepare myself for this marathon flight tomorrow.'

'As you wish.' He did not look as though it bothered him. He pulled on his cheroot, watching her with an enigmatic gleam in his eyes.

Verna tossed her head and left the room quickly. What an exasperating man he was!

But despite her protest that she needed rest, sleep was a long time in coming. Ward Levitt had crept under her skin whether she liked it or not, and it was his face that floated before her mind's eye. Always he mocked her, a derisive sneer on his lips, a calculating gleam to those brilliant blue eyes.

'Damn you!' she said over and over again. 'Why on earth did Guy have to send you? Why couldn't it have been someone a little more co-operative?'

She tossed and turned, growing hotter by the minute despite switching the air-conditioning to full. She stripped off her perspiration-soaked nightdress and had another cooling shower, then threw herself angrily down on to the bed.

'Are you all right?' Ward's voice sounded on the other side of her door.

'Perfectly well, thank you,' she tossed back loudly. 'What do you want? Don't you know what time it is?'

'Indeed I do,' came his response, and she could tell by his tone that he was smiling. 'I heard you moving about and guessed you must have difficulty in sleeping. I have some cold Brazilian fruit juice, if you would like some?'

The thought was tempting. She hesitated, then said, 'Just a minute while I find something to put on.'

'Don't bother for my benefit.'

'I might have known you'd say something like that!' she retorted, pulling a cotton housecoat over her shoulders, and belting it at the waist.

When she opened the door he drawled, 'Are you insinuating that I'm not to be trusted?'

She shrugged. 'I don't know you well enough to make such a statement.' Ward wore nothing but his hip-hugging cream trousers. His muscular chest was deeply tanned, with not an ounce of superfluous flesh, and she felt a mad impulse to run her fingers over his gleaming body. It was too perfect to be true.

'It could be rectified,' he suggested softly, his eyes raking the vee of her gown. 'It would be most uncomfortable for Guy if we were sworn enemies.

We spend a lot of time together, he and I, and I somehow think he was expecting a nice cosy threesome.'

'Then he's in for a disappointment.' She turned back into the room, resenting the way this man took control of the situation. 'I can see no way that we'll ever be friends.'

'Not even for Guy's sake? At least let's be civil in front of him.' He filled a glass with fruit juice from the jug which he carried and handed it to her.

Verna took the drink. 'There's plenty of time. Let's cross that bridge when we come to it.'

Their eyes met and held, and Verna was the first to turn away. There was something magnetic about this man that she did not understand. It was almost as though he was willing her to like him—though for what reason?

The tension in the room grew and she took a long drink from her glass. The liquid was sickly sweet, not at all what she had expected, and in no way did it assuage her thirst.

She thrust it back at him. 'It's horrid! Drink it yourself. I'll ring down for some iced water.'

He grinned unexpectedly. 'At last something on which we both agree. I don't like it either. Let's make that iced water for two, shall we? Or would you prefer something stronger? Maybe a *pinga* will help you sleep?'

She shook her head strongly. 'I hope you're not planning to get me drunk? Water will do fine, thank you.'

He shrugged easily and lifted the phone. The waiter arrived almost instantly with a tray bearing their water. Verna thought that he gave them an odd glance, and for the first time in her life she could ever remember doing so she blushed.

Inevitably Ward noticed. 'I shouldn't worry,' he mocked. 'I expect he's broadminded.'

'But we aren't doing anything?' she protested hotly.

'We know that—but the waiter—well——' He shrugged easily. 'It's understandable that he got the wrong idea. I mean, it is almost one. Most people are in bed by this time.'

Most people don't have their thoughts disturbed by irritating men like you! she wanted to yell, but she kept quiet. Antagonising him would get her nowhere.

He sat down with his drink, making himself comfortable, and she eyed him warily. 'I hope you don't intend staying. You're the important one. You at least need your sleep. I can always sleep in the plane.'

Ward shrugged easily. 'A couple of hours will do me. I thought I was doing you a favour keeping you company. Are you trying to say you want me out of here?'

It sounded rude to give him an outright yes, so she said, 'Let's say the longer you remain the less sleep I shall get.'

He sighed and pushed himself to his feet. 'And I thought my luck was in.'

She shot him a hostile glance. 'Sorry to disappoint you, Mr Levitt. It's my rule number one never to make love in hotel bedrooms.'

His lips quirked. 'Rules are made to be broken.'

Slowly he crossed so that he stood close without actually touching her. Verna's heartbeats quickened unexpectedly, but she stood her ground. No way would she let him know that he disturbed her!

She had not realised exactly how tall he was, she was forced to tilt her head to look up at him and when she did she looked away again quickly. There was something compelling about him—a sexual magnetism that could not be ignored.

Swiftly she twisted away, but his hands caught her shoulders and brought her back round to face him. 'Are you frightened of me?' he enquired softly.

She shook her head positively. 'Why should I be that? I've dated plenty of men in my time—I know how to handle them, especially if they become too amorous.'

'Meaning that you think I'm in danger of becoming precisely that now?' The question was posed with a thinly veiled threat behind it. 'Let me tell you here and now, lady, that I'm in no danger of losing my head over you.'

Yet even as he spoke his lips came down and claimed hers, and Verna could not ignore the warning bells that sounded inside her head. Her reaction was entirely unlike anything else she had ever felt. Her whole body became alive, as though she had only been half living before.

What sort of a man was he that he could do this to her? She had prided herself on always being in command of her feelings. Now she felt like flinging her arms round him and holding him close, taking all that he had to offer and giving of herself in return.

It was an odd situation, and one that she was not sure that she liked. It did not suit her to be taken over like this, and her first impulse was to struggle violently. Then she realised that this was what he expected, so instead she remained rigid, letting him kiss her, but offering no response.

He flung away, his face set, his blue eyes intense. 'A cold fish, just as I thought. Women like you are all the same.'

'What do you mean, women like me?' she demanded angrily.

'You cover up your ineptitude to make love by boasting about the previous men in your life. If the truth's known I suspect that there's never been anyone else. That one date with you is enough for any man.'

Verna had never felt so insulted in all her life. She gasped and raised her hand to strike him. But he caught it in a vice-like grip, then propelled her across the room to her bed, pushing her down mercilessly. 'Never try to hit me!' he bit out furiously.

'And don't you insult me!' she cried rashly. 'You don't know what you're talking about!' Her eyes were like twin points of fire and her breasts heaved as she fought for control. The belt had slipped from her housecoat, which slipped open to reveal a long length of thigh and the softly rounded curve of her hip.

She pulled it savagely over her. 'Get out, before I call the manager!'

Ward's temper dissolved abruptly, and as he turned towards the door he smiled. 'What would you tell him, I wonder? That you objected to giving me one simple little goodnight kiss?'

'Kisses usually lead to something else!' she yelled. 'Especially with men like you.'

'And how do you know what I'm like?' he mused, folding his arms across his powerful chest and leaning nonchalantly against the door. 'When you won't give yourself the chance to find out?'

She picked up the pillow and hurled it. 'It's typewritten all over your face.'

He grinned, sidestepping and catching the cushion easily. 'You really ought to learn to take better aim.'

'Oh, go to hell!' she snapped, deliberately averting her face from him, wishing she had never allowed herself to become involved with such an objectionable character.

'Not a very ladylike statement,' he returned, tossing the pillow back. 'I hope you don't speak to your father like that—he'd be most upset.'

'If he's the gentleman you make out, he won't treat me like you do,' she flashed.

'I give you no more than you deserve. Goodnight, little lady, pleasant dreams.'

He was gone before she could retaliate. She punched the pillow several times, silently fuming, then endeavoured to get some sleep.

As Ward had prophesied, they left Rio much later than planned. The plane was a single-engined Cessna Centurion painted a gleaming red and white. It looked well cared for, and Ward Levitt knew exactly what he was doing. Even so Verna was apprehensive, and showed it, and he seemed to take a devilish delight in her fears.

They had breakfasted early, but there had been a tension between them that Verna could not ignore. She had concentrated instead on the plate of strange-looking fruit that had been placed before them, selecting a banana, which tasted quite sweet and unlike anything she had eaten at home.

Iced tea arrived in tall frosted glasses, which Verna sipped gratefully. Even at this early hour it was unbearably hot, and already the thin trousers and cotton top she had chosen to wear were soaked with perspiration.

They had hung around the airport for a couple of hours until Ward finally announced that his plane was ready. 'Are you fit?' he asked, a wicked gleam in his eyes.

Verna glanced. 'As fit as I'll ever be, I suppose.' She climbed into the seat beside him, glancing apprehensively through the window as he checked that all was clear for take-off, closing her eyes as they taxied along the runway and holding on to the edge of her seat as they rose into the air. The small plane soared like a bird, flying over the mountains that surrounded Rio, and soon all the glamour of the city was behind them.

Ward wore jeans this morning, faded blue denim that hugged his thighs, and a checked cotton shirt, also in blue. His dark glasses hid his eyes, but Verna was aware that he glanced at her from time to time, though not once did he enquire how she was feeling.

She shrugged mentally. She really had nothing to say. 'I'm afraid there's been a slight change of plan,' he said suddenly, and she tensed, wondering what was coming next. 'I had a phone call this morning. I have to make a detour—business, you understand? This journey may take a little longer than anticipated.'

'That's all I need!' she groaned. 'Are you sure you're not doing this on purpose, knowing this trip terrifies me?'

'You think I would?' His expression was sceptical. 'I want your company no more than you want mine. It's unfortunate that two such incompatible people have been thrust together, but there's nothing we can do about it. We'll have to make the best of a difficult situation.'

'Extending the trip won't help,' she returned tightly. 'How much longer shall we be?'

He gave a dismissive gesture with his hands. 'It's difficult to say. In terms of distance, I suppose it's about another eight hundred miles.'

Verna's mouth fell open. 'You say that as though

it's nothing. But surely it means we won't get there today?'

He nodded. 'I'm as sorry as you, don't forget. I rang Guy from the hotel, and he too is disappointed.'

'Why didn't you let me speak to him?' she asked sharply.

'Because I thought it best you meet first.'

'*You* thought it best? Don't you care how I feel?'

His brows rose above the dark glasses. 'You've shown remarkably little interest so far. Why should you be any different now?'

'Oh, you're impossible!' Verna shook her head angrily and looked out of the window.

Ward laughed softly to himself and they continued their flight in silence.

She soon realised that he was a first-class pilot, and some of the tension drained out of her. He flew the plane with relaxed confidence and Verna eventually began to enjoy herself, looking down at the ever-changing scenery. Towns and villages swiftly came and went, they flew low over a river and she thought she saw crocodiles basking on its banks. She hoped she was wrong.

Several hours later they reached Brasilia, the capital of Brazil, and stopped to refuel. Verna was glad to stretch her legs and was relieved to find it slightly cooler here than in Rio.

Ward took her to a restaurant where they ate *charasco* grilled steak, and drank glasses of ice cold beer—and then they were on their way again.

Their journey now took them over bare hills and the never-ending matted green of the interior. Flocks of blue and red longtailed birds circled over tree-tops, they saw abandoned villages, and occasional meandering rivers. They spotted *rocas* being claimed back by the jungle, which Ward explained were clearings where the Indians grew manioc and maize, but which had to be abandoned after one year because the thick tangle of jungle soon began to grow again.

There were patches of open, swampy ground and they saw deer drinking from a pool. He circled low to get a closer look, but they raced back into the jungle at their approach.

Verna had closed her eyes when she suddenly became aware that the engine was no longer steadily throbbing. It gave intermittent sharp bursts of sound, as though choking, then settled down for a few more minutes before doing it all over again.

She looked at her companion quickly. There was a frown of concentration on his face and he was studying the dials intently.

'What's wrong?' She had to shout to make herself heard above the noise of the engine.

'We've lost oil pressure.' He sounded tense. 'It looks as though we might have to make an unscheduled landing. Keep your eyes open for an airstrip, they're dotted all over the place.'

Verna swallowed the terror that rose in her throat. 'What if we can't find one—is it serious—are we likely to crash in the jungle?'

He glanced at her impatiently. 'How the hell do I know? It's not unheard-of for planes to come down in this region without a trace—so you'd better keep on looking—or start praying!'

## CHAPTER THREE

THE next few minutes were the most frightening that Verna had ever spent. The tiny craft continued to splutter and choke, while she frantically searched the area for one of the rough landing strips that Ward had insisted were to be found.

'We're going to die!' she cried frantically. 'I knew it was a mistake coming all this way with you!'

*'Shut up!'* His voice was like a whiplash in the tiny cabin and she glanced at him fearfully, her face pale and perspiring profusely. She almost wished she could die, from fright, rather than go down in that jungle where who knew what fate might await them.

She felt overwhelmingly afraid and her mind was crowded with visions of dripping trees, thick undergrowth, poisonous snakes, but worst of all untamed Indians who would resent their intrusion and maybe kill them in any case if they did not die in the crash.

Nausea added to her unease and she clamped her hand over her mouth, looking at Ward with wide scared eyes.

'Heavens! You're not going to be sick?'

The scorn in his voice effectively quelled her rising panic. She looked away again hastily, scanning the thousand different greens of the jungle for the trace of a clearing that could prove their life-saver.

Then with one last choking gasp their engine died altogether, and Verna broke out into a cold sweat, swivelling her eyes to look at her companion. She was rigid with fear, her fingers curled into her palms, her back ramrod-straight. She even stopped breathing for a few seconds, before she gasped for air and turned on Ward Levitt.

'What are we going to do?' Her voice rasped into the silence.

The plane glided smoothly down, Ward's eyes probing the dense jungle beneath them. He seemed irritated that she should break his concentration. 'For God's sake keep looking. According to my calculation there's a village here somewhere—there should be a landing strip. With a bit of luck we might make it.'

They would need more than a bit of luck, thought Verna. They would require more than their fair share if they were to come out of this alive. She checked that her seat-belt was secure, wiping her sweaty palms on her damp trousers, breathing deeply and irregularly, and constantly praying.

'There!'

She followed the direction of his finger, saw a curl of smoke in the distance. They were losing height rapidly now, but the landing strip was in sight and she childishly crossed her fingers that they might come down safely. She did not fancy their chances if they landed in the jungle.

Her eyes never left Ward's face as he positioned the plane accurately. From all outward appearances he was in complete control of the situation, but she knew that inside he must be as tense as she.

Had he ever been in such a predicament before? she wondered. Or was this the first time that his supposedly reliable plane had let him down? And it had to be while she was in it!

They cleared the treetops by what must have been inches, and came to a lurching halt at the very end of the tiny runway. Verna slumped in her seat, aware that her face must be ashen, and her limbs shook so violently that she had difficulty in controlling them.

She wanted to cry, but knew instinctively that this man would condemn her for it. He came from a tough breed—and expected everyone else to be the same.

With an attempt at a laugh she said, 'That was close!'

'Mm, too close for comfort,' came his caustic rejoinder. 'You all right?'

She nodded. 'I think so. A little shaky, maybe, and relieved that we've landed in one piece.'

He took off his glasses and passed a hand over his brow. 'Did you ever have any doubts?'

'Plenty,' she returned fervently. 'What do we do now? Are you going to be able to mend the plane? How do we get out of here?'

As she spoke she looked through the window and saw to her horror that a party of Indians had gathered round the small craft, dark-skinned men with bows and arrows, their bodies coated with red paint, women with babies on their hips and children hiding behind them.

They looked a fearsome lot, and Verna instinctively clung to Ward's arm, her mouth dry and her heart thumping painfully. 'Are they friendly?' she asked in a breathless whisper, her eyes so wide they almost filled her face.

Ward shrugged characteristically. 'There's only one way to find out.' He opened his door and climbed down, smiling at the staring Indians, explaining that their plane had broken down and they had been forced to land.

Verna watched from the safety of the cabin. It became obvious that they had not the remotest idea what Ward was talking about, even though he gesticulated freely, pointing up at the plane and to Verna inside.

He beckoned her to get out, which she did hesitantly, approaching the Indians with trepidation, standing close to Ward, glad when he put his arm about her shoulders—for the first time since their meeting welcoming his attention.

He said something to them in a mixture of Portuguese and pidgin English, shrugging expressively and pointing to the plane, and eventually it seemed that they understood.

One of the men, who was obviously their chief, beckoned for them to follow him. Verna looked apprehensively at Ward. 'Is it safe?'

He grimaced ruefully. 'We haven't much choice. At least the tribe's not hostile. Not many of them are these days. I have an anthropologist friend who visits the Amerindians from time to time. He's on quite friendly terms with them and they look forward to his visits. This tribe is obviously used to the white man.'

They left the runway behind and moved into the jungle, Verna still clinging to Ward's arm, not at all sure that she believed they were not going to be eaten alive. It was much darker and cooler, though still humid, and she could smell the damp earth. It was not as thick as she had imagined it would be, although on either side of the path the trees grew close together, forming a canopy overhead. Twisted creepers like ropes hung between them and below was a thick mat of vegetation. Occasionally she caught a glimpse of blue and red fleshy flowers, relieving the all-pervading green of the jungle.

'Beware of insects dropping from the trees,' warned Ward. 'Some of them are poisonous.'

Verna wished he hadn't said anything—he was

making her even more frightened. She had never considered herself a person who was afraid of anything—certainly not in civilisation. But here, where great bushes towered above them like giants, and who knew what terrors lurked in the undergrowth, she was trembling like a jelly, quite unable to let go of Ward.

He seemed annoyingly unperturbed, strolling along, his hands in his pockets, as though he was doing nothing more than going for a Sunday afternoon walk.

'I don't know why you're so frightened,' he grinned. 'At least we'll have food and drink and somewhere to sleep.'

'Sleep?' screamed Verna. 'You don't expect me to sleep with those—those natives? I wouldn't get a wink. They might kill us while we slept!'

'Don't be melodramatic,' he scoffed. 'They're all right. We wouldn't have got this far if they had any ulterior motives.'

'How do you know?' she cried. 'They could be cannibals—who knows what fate's awaiting us?' She was almost afraid to take her eyes off the tribe of Indians who filed ahead. Admittedly they did not look as though they had any intention of eating them—they looked ridiculously happy and pleased to see their unexpected visitors, but even so, no way could she repress the shudders that ran up and down her spine.

Her light sandals were not made for this type of travel, and when a thorn pierced her toe she let out a yell.

'Damn!' exploded Ward. 'Why the hell did you have to wear those ridiculous things? Here, let me get the thorn out before it turns poisonous.'

She sat down and offered him her foot, annoyed that he should scold her when it was not her fault.

'If I'd known we were going to make a trek through the jungle, I'd have worn boots,' she declared heatedly. 'If it's anyone's fault it's yours, for not making sure your damn plane was safe. I had a feeling something like this would happen. Why on earth didn't you——'

'Shut up!' he grated loudly. 'It's happened now and there's nothing we can do about it.'

'And how are we supposed to get out of here?' she asked sarcastically. 'Have you brought a tool-kit, or are you going to wave your magic wand and all will be well?'

'Stow it,' he said, plucking out the offending thorn and then sucking her toe in case there was any poison in it. 'Stay there while I go back to the plane for my first aid kit. I'd best put a plaster on that—just in case.'

'You're not going to leave me here?' Verna felt an even worse terror rise up inside her, visions of the Indians carrying her off so that she disappeared without a trace.

'I won't be a minute,' he said impatiently. 'What the hell's the matter with you, Verna? In London you were the one in command. Where's your control?'

She could have said, 'I lost it when the plane developed engine trouble.' But what would be the use? It would give him great delight to see her as the helpless female. She had never been one of those in her life.

Independence, that was what her mother had taught her. With an effort she firmed her chin, looking at him bravely. 'You're right, of course—I'm being an idiot. Go on, I'll sit here,' though she could not resist adding, 'but don't be long.'

He smiled swiftly, a warm smile which made her feel better. But as soon as he was out of sight panic rose in her throat again. The Indians had stopped to see what was happening and now came back towards her, surrounding her in a circle.

She indicated her toe, miming pain, and then pointed towards the plane, hoping they would understand what she was trying to tell them. One of the women dropped down to look at her foot, smiling broadly, and soon they were all looking to see exactly what was the trouble.

Apart from a bead of blood, there was nothing, and Verna began to feel something of a fraud. But Ward had told her to remain where she was, and she was sensible enough to realise the danger of infection if she attempted to put her foot to the ground.

The naked bodies of the women were as smooth as silk, and they had a natural grace which Verna could not help but admire. They touched her clothes, and were fascinated by her blonde curls.

The men stood a few paces back, also naked, but their bodies adorned with sticky red paint. Around their waists were beaded belts, feathered bands adorned their upper arms and their calves were wrapped with strips of material.

They all carried bows and arrows and she wondered whether they were a hunting party, disturbed by their plane, or whether they always carried these weapons.

It was a relief when Ward returned. He grinned at her obvious embarrassment, then quickly bathed her wound and pressed on a strip of plaster.

'That should do it,' he said. 'I expect these Indians think we're making a fuss over nothing, but you can't be too careful in the jungle.'

Verna allowed him to help her to her feet. 'You've been here before, then? Are you trying to tell me that it's not the first time your plane's developed engine trouble?'

His sigh was quick and impatient. 'Yes, I have been here before, and no, my plane's always been perfectly reliable up till now. I do apologise that it had to happen while you were with me.'

His dry tone put her in the wrong, and she knew she was being unreasonable, but she was damned if she was going to apologise. She shrugged and forged on ahead, ignoring him now, following the chattering Indians with determined resolve.

Soon they came to a clearing, where crops of some sort grew, and around its perimeter were several round huts with straw roofs. At their approach thin unkempt dogs rushed out, teeth bared, barking ferociously.

Verna stopped abruptly, but a word from one of the men soon had the dogs under control. They lay down outside the huts, but Verna could not help notice that they never once took their eyes off her or Ward.

More children appeared, bright eyes curious, laughing and shouting, gesticulating at the newcomers. Verna turned back to Ward, suddenly in the need of his moral support.

From his pocket he withdrew a packet of cigarettes and handed them round to the men, who accepted eagerly, their dark eyes avidly alight at this unexpected gift. *'Cigarros!'* they said loudly, puffing the smoke quickly and delightedly.

Verna wore a thin gold chain round her neck, and one of the women, who had been eyeing it surreptitiously ever since she saw it, reached out and tried to pull it from Verna's neck.

'Give it to her,' said Ward. 'It's the least we can do for their hospitality.'

'We didn't ask for it,' she returned, reluctant

to part with the expensive necklace.

'They didn't ask for us to drop out of the skies,' he replied irritably. 'Don't be so hostile, Verna. If it means so much to you I'll buy you another when we get to Belém.'

'*If* we get to Belém, don't you mean?' It hurt to part with it as if it were of no more value than a string of glass beads.

'There you go again!' There was a flash of annoyance on his face. 'Consider yourself lucky that we're alive, lady. For God's sake don't start to count the cost in terms of loss of personal possessions which can easily be replaced.'

'I wouldn't expect you to understand,' she muttered, releasing the clasp and handing the necklace to the brown grasping fingers of the Indian girl, who at once fastened it around her own slender neck, displaying it with pride to the other members of the tribe.

'I suppose if they said they wanted the clothes off my back you'd say let them have them,' she muttered testily to Ward, unable to forget her indignance at being forced to part with the chain.

'Then at least you'd be on a par,' he grinned unashamedly. 'Don't you feel somewhat over-dressed?'

She eyed the gleaming naked bodies of the Amerindians. 'Each to his own,' she said stiffly.

The chief, a young man, taller than the rest, his hair hanging long and straight, with a wide fringe, beckoned to Ward to follow him into one of the huts. Again an unreasonable terror took hold of Verna, and it was all she could do to stop herself hanging on to his arm and holding him back. She did not want to be left alone with these grasping women.

When she herself was propelled into another of

the huts she felt like screaming with a fear that sent prickles down her spine. Not once had she imagined, when embarking on this trip to Brazil, that anything like this would happen to her. You saw such things in films, or read about it in books, but for it to happen in real life, was more than she could accept. Her eyes were wide and scared and she felt close to real panic.

Yet inside was a scene of perfect domesticity. The hut was cool and airy, babies lay in hammocks quite contentedly, their soft eyes watchful. A woman held a baby to her breast, and another stirred something in a pot over a fire at the end of the room.

Other women were preparing food and children played on the floor—all contented, not one of them crying or vying for attention. More dogs eyed her suspiciously, and there were baskets piled high with all sorts of dried food.

Guns and bows and arrows were hung high, out of the reach of the children and a pair of parakeets squabbled in harsh cackling voices.

They indicated that she should sit on the floor and she watched with interest as they prepared the food for cooking, peeling the dark skin off what looked like peculiar shaped vegetables, shredding the flesh through wooden graters, squeezing out the juice, and then shaping the resultant dough into flat cakes.

Another girl pounded maize in a wooden pestle.

By the time Ward came to find her she had forgotten her fears and was playing with one of the children, drawing pictures on the dirt floor with a stick.

'We've been allocated a hut,' he told her, 'until I can fix the plane. Come and look.'

With the child still clinging to her hand Verna followed Ward. The hut was small in comparison to the one she had been in, with two hammocks slung from poles, a table, but very little else.

'Do they expect me to sleep here, with you?' she questioned, feeling fiery colour burn her cheeks. 'Couldn't we have separate rooms?'

'What do you think this is, the Ritz?' he questioned, his eyes amused. 'You should be thankful they don't expect us to join them. How would you fancy undressing in front of that lot?'

'About as little as I relish doing it in front of you!' she returned tightly.

'Now's not the time to think about modesty.' His lips quirked as he spoke and she could tell that he really quite enjoyed the situation.

She flashed him a hostile glance. 'How long do you reckon we're going to be stuck here?'

He lifted his shoulders expressively. 'Your guess is as good as mine. Until I've had an opportunity to assess what's wrong with the plane I can't tell you.'

'And when are you likely to do that?' she flared swiftly.

'In the morning. By the time we've eaten it will be dark.' He glanced down at the chuckling boy who clung to Verna's hand. 'You've made a conquest there. Think you can keep yourself occupied while I fetch some of our things from the plane?'

'Can't I come with you?' she pleaded at once.

He shook his head. 'I'll be quicker alone. You have nothing at all to worry about. Why don't you go back and help the women cook the meal?'

'It's not my type of cooking, but I will admit they're not so bad as I at first thought. I'll take laughing boy here back, before they think I've abducted him.'

The women looked up as Verna entered the hut, smiling quickly, and then ignoring her as they continued with their preparations. Very soon she had a whole crowd of children round her as she drew pictures on the dusty floor, and Ward was back before she had really had time to miss him.

They ate their meal in yet another hut, sitting round a long table. There were dishes of rice, and tough stewed chicken. The manioc bread, which a girl had been making, and which Ward told her was a staple part of their diet, and floury brown beans, which were also another food which was eaten at every meal.

There were fresh limes which they cut in half and squeezed into thick wooden cups filled with water, and to her surprise Verna found that she quite enjoyed it, for she was starving.

Ward handed round more cigarettes, and she began to wonder whether he was always so well prepared. Perhaps, living in his country, one had to be, though she was quite sure that had she known what was in store she would not have come.

As he had prophesied, it was dark by the time they had finished. They went to their own hut and Ward sat outside while she undressed by the light from a torch which he had suspended from the ceiling.

She had never before realised how tricky it was climbing into a hammock, and it took several attempts before she finally managed to ease herself in safely. It was not until then that she realised she wanted to go to the lavatory.

'Go round the back of the hut,' advised Ward when he came in and she told him of her dilemma, 'but keep moving your feet in case of ants and things.'

Verna had never before completed such a quick toilet, and she dived back into the hut, wondering how on earth she was going to manage if they were stuck here in the jungle for any length of time.

Ward switched off the torch and undressed in the darkness. Somewhere close a mosquito buzzed, and Verna was glad of the mosquito net that Ward had miraculously provided.

Earlier on he had given her an anti-malaria pill. 'You must have one every day,' he told her.

'Are you always so well prepared?' she asked scathingly, annoyed that there seemed to be nothing that this man could not provide. She should be grateful, yet somehow his competence irritated her.

'For any contingency,' he replied drily. 'You have a lot to learn, little lady. This is not England now, you know. This is wild country where anything, but anything, can happen.'

She lay in silence now, watching the red end of his cigar as he lay relaxed in his hammock. Very soon there was silence and the deep rhythm of his breathing told her that he was asleep.

But sleep for Verna was a sheer impossibility. The mosquitoes that had been droning round their hut managed to find their way beneath her netting and she felt several bites on her arms and legs, which began to itch uncontrollably.

She was hot and uncomfortable and becoming increasingly irate by the second. In the end she could stand it no longer. 'Ward,' she whispered, and then more loudly, 'Ward!'

From somewhere in the darkness came his voice. 'Go to sleep, damn you. You'll be good for nothing in the morning.'

'I'm good for nothing now,' she snapped. 'I've been bitten all over by these pesky mosquitoes. Let's go to the plane and sleep there, I'm sure it'll be better.'

'I'm not moving,' he said. 'You go if you like.'

He must have known she would not go without him. 'Please,' she begged. 'I'm so uncomfortable!'

'You'd be a darned sight more uncomfortable in the plane,' he replied. 'You'd be compelled to sleep next to me, for one thing, and I can hardly see you accepting that.'

Anything would be preferable to this hammock, she thought, but he could be right. She had forgotten how confined the cabin space was. 'Can't you do anything about these mosquitoes?' she asked plaintively, slapping her leg as yet another of them bit her.

She heard him sigh and move around, and the next moment the torch cast a beam of light into the darkness. He took one look at her and said scornfully, 'What do you expect, wearing a thing like that?'

Verna looked down at her short cotton nightdress. 'What's wrong with it?'

'You need to be covered up,' he replied, 'from head to toe.'

She noticed that his pyjamas were closely buttoned, with elastic bands at both the wrist and ankle.

'Thanks for telling me,' she replied scathingly.

'You scuttled into bed so quickly I hardly had time to see you,' he returned impatiently. He searched in his suitcase and brought out another pair of pyjamas, pushing them into her hands together with a tube of ointment. 'Here, cover yourself with that and get into these. Perhaps then we'll get a good night's sleep.'

He heaved himself back into his hammock and left her to get on with it. Verna looked at his broad back and realised that there was nothing she could do but strip off right here, and hope he would have the decency not to look.

The ointment certainly eased the itching and Ward's pyjamas were long enough to cover both her hands and her feet. Eventually she switched off the torch and climbed precariously back into her hammock. 'Goodnight, Ward, and thanks,' she whispered into the darkness.

There was no answer. He was once again fast asleep.

## CHAPTER FOUR

WHEN Verna awoke Ward's hammock was empty. There was a slight smell of cigar smoke, but that was all.

She lowered herself gingerly, aching all over, her mosquito bites swollen and itching. She felt decidedly uncomfortable and would have given anything for a long hot, scented bath.

Dragging off his pyjamas, she prayed fervently that he would get the plane going today. She did not think she could stand another night like this last one.

Suddenly she became aware that she had an audience. Through the cracks in the wooden structure of the hut half a dozen pair of eyes were watching her!

Frantically she dragged on a pair of jeans and a tee-shirt, feeling acutely embarrassed at this invasion of her privacy. When she pushed open the door the group of young Indian men and women grinned unashamedly.

Verna searched the area for Ward, giving them a half smile, but preferring to pretend that she had not seen them. Annoyingly he was nowhere in sight. Just like him! she thought angrily.

When he eventually appeared his hair was smooth and wet and shining, slicked back from his face. He looked incredibly refreshed and ready to face the new day.

'Where have you been?' she demanded. 'How dare you leave me on my own!'

'I didn't think you would thank me for waking

you,' he said with characteristic carelessness, his blue eyes watching her closely. 'I've been for a swim. The water's fresh and cool, you should go.'

'No, thanks,' she tossed disdainfully, at the same time aware that it sounded terribly tempting—and she had not had a wash since leaving Rio yesterday morning!

Then one of the girls, a long-legged beauty with the slender grace of a model, and hauntingly attractive slanting eyes, caught hold of her hand and indicated for her to follow.

Ward tossed her the tablet of soap. 'Would you like me to join you? I know you don't like being alone with these Indians.'

His taunting mockery made her eyes flash angrily. 'I'd prefer it if you went and saw to the plane.'

'Breakfast first,' he said. 'No man can work on an empty stomach.'

'Is that all you can think of?' she ventured, before being pulled away by the eager Indian.

The girl must have been somewhere near her own age, yet she seemed younger—eager and full of life, running swiftly between the huts, leading the way to where the ground fell away and a river shimmered in the heat.

It formed a natural pool, with tiny beaches, and there were several other families bathing in the coolness of the water.

Verna lost no time in stripping off her clothes, conscious not of her nakedness but of her lily-white skin compared to the brown bodies of the Amerindians.

She washed herself thoroughly all over and then, tossing the soap to the shore, spent a pleasant half hour swimming with the others, playing happily, splashing water, completely in harmony despite their inability to speak each other's language.

The company was mixed, yet in no way did she feel shy. It was something that was completely unexpected, this oasis of tranquillity in the jungle. Parakeets flew overhead, butterflies fluttered about them. It was a time Verna would always remember.

Breakfast consisted of a thick sort of soup made from manioc and pieces of dried fish which were filling if not appetising.

She then accompanied Ward to the plane, convinced that soon he would have repaired the engine and they would be on their way again. But although he toiled over it for several long, sweat-grimed hours, he was unable to fix it.

'It's no good,' he said at length. 'It needs new oil filters. They were supposed to have been replaced. Someone's going to get a rocket!'

'How are you going to get those?' she asked grimly. She was soaked to the skin in perspiration, hungry and itching, and unable to contemplate what the future held in store.

She had been certain the engine failure was a minor fault. She had relied on Ward—and he had let her down! Suddenly she began to cry, silent tears that slid down her face, mingling with the sweat and dirt.

Ward took one look at her and exploded. 'For heaven's sake, that's all I need! Trust a woman to cry at a time like this! Do you think it'll help?'

She shook her head. 'I can't help it, I'm sorry. I had faith in you.'

'Not enough, obviously,' he said, giving the plane a vicious kick. 'The damned, stupid thing! What a hell of a time to land me in trouble. Guy will be worried out of his mind when we don't turn up on time.'

'*Guy* will be worried,' she cried irrationally. 'Is that all you care about? How about me? Don't you care that you've landed me in this green hellhole?'

His brows rose savagely. 'It could be worse, Verna—far worse. Thank your lucky stars that we came down where we did. At least we're safe.'

'But we can't *stay* here,' she protested, 'not indefinitely.'

'That's right,' he said. 'We shall have to move on.'

'You mean—walk, through the jungle?' She looked at him incredulously. 'I'd never make it. I'm not cut out for this type of life.'

He smiled annoyingly. 'Then you'll have to learn. Verna Pemberton, the intrepid explorer—how does that sound?'

She did not find it funny. 'I would prefer to wait. Someone will find us, eventually. They'll discover we're missing and search the area.'

'Which could take days, or weeks, and if they don't spot the plane they'll give up. We'd be far better off trying to make our own way to one of the posts that have been set up for the protection of Indians. They'll be able to send a radio message from there.'

'You have a wireless on the plane,' she said swiftly, suddenly remembering. 'Why don't you use it?'

'Because, my dear lady, that is kaput as well. Credit me with some intelligence—that's the first thing I thought of. I tried it last night and again this morning, but it doesn't work.'

Her tears sprang swiftly to the surface again. Ward sighed deeply, impatiently, and took her into his arms. 'Verna, please, I'm as choked as you are about this whole affair.'

'B-but we could d-die in this jungle, and I'm not ready to die yet!'

'No, no.' He smoothed her hair back from her shiny brow. 'I'm a good Boy Scout; I won't let anything happen to you.' He grinned reassuringly. 'Trust me?'

She looked up into his eyes which were the same intense blue as the sky above. Her life was in the hands of this man—this comparative stranger, who had been doing no more than a favour for his friend.

It was wrong of her to blame him. He was as sick as she about the whole thing. She managed a weak smile and nodded, not realising how young and pathetic she looked.

Ward groaned and crushed her against him, and when she lifted her face wonderingly he kissed her. His lips tasted salt beneath her own, and there was something slightly insane about being kissed by this man in the middle of the Brazilian jungle.

Whether it was the heat that affected her, she did not know, but she clung unashamedly to him, returning his kisses with a desperation that could only have been conceived by their predicament. No other way would she have reacted like this.

The coolness with which she generally treated men was forgotten. Their overheated bodies pressed close, his lean powerful thighs against her own. She was aware of his heart hammering in his chest, and her own echoing in response.

When his hand cupped her breast, sliding beneath the thin material of her tee-shirt, she made no demur. There was something primitive about being here in the jungle, it changed her sense of values. She felt like a primeval woman, uninhibited, ready to accept this man with an animal passion that matched his own—and surprised herself. She had not been aware that such fires existed in her—and the only excuse she could find was that their surroundings had a lot to do with it. Had everything to do with it, in fact.

Her body pulsed with a desire that she found alarming, and with a strangled cry she abruptly pushed him from her. 'I must be crazy,' she muttered, her eyes wide. 'Why did you do that?'

'Not crazy,' he smiled, 'merely following the instincts of nature. This is wild country, behavioural patterns alter accordingly.'

'Mine don't.' She lifted her chin determinedly. 'I shan't let it happen again.'

'You may not be able to stop it.'

'Meaning that you intend to take advantage because of this unfortunate situation—that's all your fault!' Her voice rose and she stared at him like a woman demented.

'Meaning nothing of the kind,' he rasped. 'And if I'd had any choice I'd have got you to Guy Pemberton's in double quick time.'

'You saw fit to make a detour.' Her breathing was irregular, she could still feel the imprint of his lips on her own. Angrily she wiped the back of her hand across her mouth. 'If we'd gone straight to Belém we wouldn't have come down in this Godforsaken place.'

He inclined his head gravely. 'True, but it could have been worse. At least we landed in one piece.'

She looked wildly around her. 'Who knows what's lurking out there—and yet you expect me to join you, to forge our way through that—impenetrable mass, instead of waiting with the Indians until we're discovered.'

He shrugged easily. 'Very well, you wait. I'll make my way alone. I'll send someone to get you just as soon as I am able.'

*'No!'* Hysterically she clung to him. 'No, Ward, I won't let you leave me. You can't!'

'Then you have no choice.'

She eyed him begrudgingly. 'I hate you, Ward Levitt—more than I thought it possible to hate any man!'

For several long seconds he stared at her, then shrugging, he turned away. She had no recourse but to follow, all the time staring furiously at his broad back, his sweat-soaked shirt clinging to powerful muscles, revealing his tremendous physical strength.

If she was honest with herself, he was certainly the sort of man to have around in an emergency. She would be a fool to allow foolish pride to stand between her and doing what he thought best.

When they arrived at the circle of huts he headed straight to the one which had been their sleeping quarters last night. Verna followed hesitantly into the shady interior.

He stripped of his shirt and jeans, without a qualm. Beneath them he wore a pair of swimming trunks.

'I'm going to clean up,' he said, 'and then I'm off. If you want to come with me make sure that you're ready.'

She nodded miserably. 'I'm coming—I couldn't bear it waiting here. I'll take a swim too, if you don't mind?' The thick choking heat made her feel faint—the thought of bathing in the river was far too tantalising to be ignored.

She walked behind him, like the Indians did their men, feeling strangely humble, and very close again to tears. At the water's edge she stripped off to her bra and pants, and dived cleanly into the cooling depths.

After several minutes of vigorous swimming she felt better. Ward was right, of course. He always was—damn him! She gave him a half smile as she walked out of the water, unconscious of her semi-nakedness, intent only on reassuring him that she had been behaving ridiculously.

'I'm sorry,' she said, 'for being childish. It's unlike me. It must be the heat.'

'Forget it,' he returned gruffly, his eyes flicking over her, then the next second he was striding away towards the camp. Verna pulled on her jeans, her body already dry from the powerful rays of the sun, and dragged her tee-shirt over her head as she ran after him.

'Don't be angry with me,' she said. 'If there's to be just you and me I don't think I could stand it if you weren't speaking.'

He looked at her obliquely. 'You should have thought of that earlier. I have enough on my mind without pandering to hysterical females.'

'Oh!' She stamped her foot angrily. 'I might have known I couldn't appeal to your better nature!'

'That's right,' he said tightly. 'So if you want to keep on my good side you'd best do as I say without any argument—at all times!'

Verna clamped her lip tightly between her teeth to stop herself slinging back an insult. Who the hell did he think he was? But she knew that she had to defer to his judgment—he knew the jungle better than she. Or at least he pretended to. Whether it was all one big bluff for her benefit she had no way of knowing. And she did not intend to question it; she was frightened enough as it was.

At the camp he produced a haversack. 'We need to travel light,' he said. 'Put only your necessities into here. The rest you'll have to leave.'

'My new clothes?' She was aghast and prepared to argue—until she saw the grim lines on his face.

'Shirts and underclothes,' he said. 'That's all—

and an extra pair of stout shoes—if you have any? You'll have to make do with the trousers you've got on.'

'And you?' she demanded angrily. 'What are you going to take?'

He did not bother to answer, but stuffed their clothes into the haversack together with the first aid kit. He pushed a gun into his belt and handed a smaller one silently to her. She stared at it in horror. 'What's that for?'

'First rule of the jungle,' he replied calmly, 'is that you never go anywhere unarmed.'

'But I can't shoot, I've never even handled a gun!'

With patience that she found surprising Ward took her outside and gave her a half hour's lesson, so that by the time he was finished she was able to hit a cigarette packet with reasonable accuracy from about twenty paces.

But she did not like the idea, and the thought of the gun tucked away in the bottom of her handbag filled her with terror. She hoped she never needed to use it.

They had one last meal with the Indians, and it was then that they offered to let them have a canoe. 'We'll make better headway down the river,' said Ward happily. 'It's very good of them.'

'I hope it'll be safe!' Verna was not too enamoured with the idea. Thoughts of crocodiles sent shudders through her body.

'Is anything safe to you?' he questioned drily. 'You know what the alternative is.'

She said nothing after that, but was near to breaking point as they left behind the friendly Indians. It felt like the end of the road. She was quite sure they would never come out of all this alive.

She had argued that they could take more clothes since they had transport, but Ward had told her it was impossible, that although part of their journey would be by boat, they would still have plenty of walking to do.

The boat, cut from a tree trunk, was old and to Verna's wary eye looked totally unreliable. She had visions of them sinking slowly, trying to fight off with their paddles the snapping alligators who waited for this unexpected meal.

She sat down in the bottom, waving to the grinning Indians as Ward paddled his way down the River Xingu. Soon the band of people were out of sight and they were alone.

She could think of nothing to say, watching the thick jungle which fringed the edge of the water, so tangled and dense that it looked impenetrable.

Occasionally the sides of the river rose in high walls of mud, at others where it widened out there were sandbanks, and Ward pointed out the foot-marks of the alligators.

As if she wasn't frightened enough!

In places brilliant coloured kingfishers darted along the banks, great white herons flew ahead and brown and white striped butterflies fluttered above their heads.

It was suffocatingly hot and Verna plastered her face with sun lotion. One of the Indian girls had given her a straw hat which protected her head to some extent, but even so the sun's rays were un-bearable.

'How far do we have to go like this?' she asked at length. The river was faster flowing here and Ward was able to sit back and rest and let the current take them along.

'As far as we can,' he said pragmatically. 'The river goes for hundreds of miles, but I somehow doubt we'll get that far.' He smiled as he spoke, to soften his words.

Verna grimaced, dipped her handkerchief in the water and tried to cool her burning face. 'It's unbearable. I don't think I can put up with it for much longer. Is anywhere on earth quite so hot? It's like being in a Turkish bath.'

'It is pretty uncomfortable,' he agreed, 'If it's any consolation I think you're bearing up remarkably well.'

Praise indeed! She looked at him warily, wondering whether he was merely saying that to make her feel better. But he looked sincere, 'Thanks,' she said. 'But I can't promise I won't suddenly go berserk.'

In the depths of the jungle they heard a troop of monkeys chattering loudly and noisily and she felt like joining them, screaming her head off, begging to be taken out of here.

'I'd love a swim,' she said suddenly. 'Couldn't we stop at one of those sandbanks?'

'Not if you don't want to be eaten alive.' Ward quirked a brow comically. 'The water's full of piranha, not to mention alligators.'

Verna repressed a shudder and changed her mind rapidly, her eyes now fixed on the murky green-grey depths for any sight of these man-eating monsters.

They travelled for over three hours before Ward suggested they stop to eat. Verna was relieved. She ached with sitting in the hard wooden bottom of the boat and longed to stretch her legs.

Even so she was wary at leaving the relative safety of their canoe, and she climbed out carefully her eyes all the time watchful for danger. There were no telltale marks on the sandbank, though, and she walked about energetically, stretching her arms and legs, and finally lying full length on the sand.

From the depths of his haversack Ward magically produced a tiny Primus over which he boiled water and cooked rice which the Indians had given to him. This, together with pieces of dried meat, was their lunch, followed by scalding cups of coffee.

'Not much, I'm afraid,' he said, as he sat back later relaxing on the sand. 'I'll catch some fish for supper.'

Verna said nothing, busy cleaning their wooden plates with handfuls of sand, and repacking everything into the haversack. She was not cut out for this type of life, she was sure. She preferred to sit down to a good meal, not rely on whatever they might be able to catch or shoot.

But she was determined not to argue with Ward. Falling out with him now would make the journey doubly unendurable. The annoying part was that he seemed to be quite enjoying it. Never once had he shown any signs of exhaustion, even though he had been paddling their canoe for almost the whole of the time they had been travelling.

He was a giant of a man, tough as whipcord, making every job look easy. Lesser men would have given up before now. No way would they have been able to withstand this enervating, cloying heat.

Drawing in breaths of air was like inhaling the steam in a sauna, yet Ward lay there, outwardly composed, even humming softly to himself, smoking a cheroot and in complete harmony with his surroundings.

'What sort of work do you do?' she asked suddenly. It could be no easy job, or he would not be in such a superb state of physical fitness.

He looked at her lazily. 'Is that idle talk, or do you really want to know?'

'I wouldn't have asked, if I didn't,' she replied sharply, and wished she had been less hasty. It was this heat that made her snappish. She tempered her words with, 'I really would like to know. I'm curious about you. You take all this in your stride, as though it's nothing. To me it's the end of the world.'

He smiled. 'I don't think so. It's surprising what anyone can do if they have to. You'll survive.'

'I wish I had your confidence.' She linked her hands round her knees and looked at him, reluctant to admit, even to herself, that she admired Ward Levitt. She had never met anyone quite like him before. The way he relaxed now anyone would think they were out for an afternoon picnic, rather than fighting for survival in the Brazilian jungle.

'It's a case of adapting,' he told her. 'Worry won't help. One way or another we've got to get ourselves out of this. If you're determined to win, you will, no matter what the odds.'

'How long do you reckon it will take us?'

He grimaced wryly. 'It's impossible to say. On my own I could do it in a couple of days, but——'

'With me to hinder you, it will take much longer?' she finished for him. 'I'm sorry if I'm not the explorer type. It comes as a shock when you suddenly have it thrust upon you.'

'You'll look back on this and laugh.' He finished his cigar, flicking the end into the river, and jumping to his feet. 'Are you fit?'

He extended his hand, and she took it willingly. She felt so weak it was unbelievable. For a few seconds he looked into her eyes and she thought he was going to kiss her again. Her breathing stilled and her pulses leaped unexpectedly.

Then as suddenly he let her go, and stepped into the canoe, leaving her to clamber in herself. She sensed an anger inside him, and wondered why.

With fierce energy Ward paddled the canoe downstream. His face set and determined and another couple of hours passed without either of them speaking.

The heat from the sun became even more unendurable and Verna felt close to fainting, only sheer determination not to weaken in front of Ward making her hang on to consciousness.

She reached one of the cups out of the haversack and poured water over herself in a futile attempt to keep cool. Soon she was conscious that Ward was watching the riverbanks closely and she wondered whether he was looking for somewhere to camp the night. Her watch had given up earlier that day, but her stomach told her that it was time for something to eat, and she joined him in his search for a break in the dense vegetation which would allow them to stop well away from the water's edge.

Suddenly the trees thinned. Ward slowed down, and finally stopped the canoe alongside the bank.

Although the undergrowth was less thick, he was still compelled to hack his way through with a sharp knife. He really was prepared for all eventualities, she thought. Was there any obstacle he could not surmount?

She followed with the haversack, feeling useless, surprised when they came upon a small clearing that looked as though it was purpose-made for camping.

'Shall I light the Primus?' she asked, after she had emptied the haversack of their meagre food supply. Her stomach was protesting loudly.

'I'll light a fire,' he said, cutting wood.

Her brows shot up. 'It will be quicker using the stove. I'm starving!'

'And I suppose I'm not?' he bit back. 'Use your sense, woman. We must preserve what we've got for emergencies.'

And this wasn't one? Verna sighed angrily. 'What would you like me to do, then? Rub two sticks together and light the damn thing?'

His blue eyes were coldly angry. 'You're hot and hungry, but getting cross is not going to help.' Expertly he piled the sticks into a pyramid, pushed in a handful of dried grass and twigs, and soon had the fire burning brightly.

'You can get water,' he told her, 'for the rice and coffee. I'm going to see if I can catch some fish.'

The red ball of the sun was sinking below the horizon in a blaze of unforgettable colour. Orange, gold and red streaked the sky, to change almost immediately into softer pinks and yellows before the glow faded altogether. Verna stood entranced, for the moment her discomfort forgotten.

Then she saw Ward standing in the bows of the boat, dangling a line into the water, and she filled her pans with water and hurried back to their camp before he could chastise her again for wasting time.

When he shouted triumphantly she guessed he had had a bite—and a few minutes later he strode into the clearing with about four fish strung together.

'Your supper,' he said proudly.

Verna grinned, her earlier anger forgotten. 'Thank goodness, I can't last much longer. What are they?'

'Piranha,' he said, as though it was obvious, and

at her disgusted expression, 'They're good. Are you going to clean them or shall I?'

'You,' she said quickly. 'I'll make the coffee. The rice is almost ready.'

Deftly he chopped off the fishes' tales, and their heads, with mouthfuls of teeth that made Verna realise how easily they could savage a human being, then slit them open and sliced out the bones.

Soon a delicious smell of smoked fish filled the air and Verna could hardly wait to begin eating. She gave not a thought to the fact that it was piranha as she hungrily devoured the contents of her plate.

'It is good,' she said to Ward, as she wiped her plate clean with a portion of manioc bread. 'What's for afters?'

'If you want to go into the jungle and see what you can find, you're welcome,' he smiled. 'So far as I'm concerned, I'm going to sleep just as soon as we've cleaned up.'

No way did Verna fancy going into the jungle alone, so she gave up the idea of some exotic fresh fruit and helped Ward tidy away their utensils instead.

'Where do we sleep?' she asked at length. The floor was alive with ants, black stinging insects that had already bitten her more times than she could count. They had eaten their meal standing up.

Now Ward pulled from the bottom of his magical bag a couple of hammocks which he slung between the trees. 'Your bed awaits you,' he said with mock dignity.

Verna flashed him a wide smile. 'Is there nothing you can't supply?'

'I try to be prepared,' he said simply. 'One learns in a country like this that it's better to have and not need than to be caught out. It's a form of insurance.'

'I'm grateful,' she said. 'I'd like to swill my hands and face before I go to sleep. Is it safe to go down to the river?'

'It's only a few yards,' he laughed, 'and so long as you don't wade out too far so that the piranhas get you——'

'There's no fear of that,' she replied strongly. 'I've never felt so sweaty and dirty in all my life, but nothing will get me into that water!'

He handed her a torch. 'Here, take this. Would you like me to come with you?'

She would, but she needed privacy at that moment, so she shook her head firmly. 'I can manage.'

At first she did not see the long black shapes at the water's edge and walked confidently across the sand, shining her torch on the ground immediately in front of her.

It was not until she swung the beam into a wider circle that she saw the torpedo-like objects zooming in on her—black and scaly with glowing red eyes—and when she realised that she could have walked unsuspectingly right in among them, she froze from sheer terror.

A scream rose in her throat, but it was a long time before she heard the thin wail of her own voice, seeming to come from a long distance away.

# CHAPTER FIVE

WARD reached Verna's side in a matter of seconds, his gun at the ready. She had never been so pleased to see him in all her life. She turned into his arms and clung desperately. 'You said I'd be all right,' she sobbed. 'I never dreamt there'd be crocodiles. Oh, Ward, I'm so scared.'

'Don't be,' he said, leading her calmly back to the camp. 'You're not hurt, so why all the fuss? Time for that when you're really in danger. And they're alligators, not crocodiles!'

She pushed him away from her. 'Are you trying to say that I wasn't in danger? I could have been eaten alive! Their jaws were enormous, I'd have been gone in one swallow. And you say don't make a fuss!'

'Did you really see their mouths?' he laughed. 'They seemed to be swimming around quite amiably to me. I've seen some really dangerous fellows in my time, thrashing and snapping so that no one can get near them. I can assure you you'd really be scared then.'

Verna shook her head angrily. 'Oh! It's all a game to you, isn't it? You think it's funny!'

'Have I said that?' The intenseness of his eyes disturbed her. 'Surviving in the jungle is no fun, I can assure you, but it does become a game. Why take life seriously? It's far too short for that. If you can see humour in a situation, why not, I say.'

'Huh!' Verna was far from pacified. 'You wouldn't be saying that if you were in my position!'

'I'd be drinking in all that was new and exciting,'

he said. 'Storing it in my memory. Who knows, you could become famous. I can just see the headlines—Woman survives against all odds. Bravery of Verna Pemberton, etcetera, etcetera.'

Despite herself Verna had to laugh. 'Don't be a fool! *If* I survive all credit will go to you. I'm a coward, and I'll admit it.'

'No, you're not. Come on, let me help you into your hammock.'

It was quite a game trying to struggle in beneath the folds of the mosquito net without letting any of the vicious little insects in as well, but eventually Verna made it, and she gave Ward a triumphant smile when she was finally settled. 'Goodnight,' she called, 'and thanks.'

'Don't mention it,' he quipped.

Through the gauze of the mosquito net she could see him smoking one last cheroot before he too turned in, and it was comforting to know that he was out there.

Eventually all that could be heard was the fire crackling and the night noises of the jungle. Hundreds of insects hummed, and crickets and frogs kept up a continual throbbing. Howler monkeys yelled in the distance and in the undergrowth it sounded as though a whole army of little animals were on the move. Verna was reluctant to close her eyes.

But she did drop off, waking once to see Ward stoking up the fire. He looked in her direction and moved towards her, then clearly thinking better of it returned to his own hammock.

Verna made no noise. He did not even know she was awake. She wondered what he had been going to do, but before long sleep claimed her again and when she next woke it was light and Ward's hammock had disappeared.

The fire burned brightly and there was an appetising smell of fish once again. Ward squatted on his haunches before it and when Verna eventually rolled out of her hammock he had their breakfast ready.

'Sorry for the monotony of the diet,' he said, an eyebrow quirking, daring her to complain. 'I'll try and think of something different for lunch.'

'I couldn't care less what it is,' said Verna. 'I'm ravenous! Why didn't you wake me? I'd have cooked the breakfast. I feel as though I'm a drag on you. You must make me pull my weight.'

He grinned, his teeth white in the darkness of his face. 'There'll be plenty of time for that. We've had it easy so far. Make the most of it while you can.'

There was something ominous about the way he spoke, but Verna was afraid to question him. It was best she did not know what was in store.

An hour later they were on their way again. The sun was already high in the sky and she felt her skin begin to burn. She covered herself with her quickly diminishing supply of sun cream, irritated that the sun should not affect her companion. His skin was tanned to a smooth deep shade of mahogany, with only a few lines, not wrinkled as she would imagine a person's skin to be after spending innumerable hours in this intense heat.

They made good progress, and Verna began to feel happier. She was getting used to their somewhat primitive form of travelling, and with Ward for a companion, who could be afraid?

But suddenly the sky darkened and she looked at him, her eyes wide and expressive.

'An electric storm,' he told her. 'These tropical storms whip up from nowhere and although they're fierce they don't last.'

She scanned the banks feverishly for somewhere to stop and shelter, but the alternate high sides and flat sandbanks afforded no protection—and so they kept on.

The grey clouds which formed were beautifully shaped and at first fascinated Verna, but as they darkened, and great rolls of thunder reverberated through the air, interspersed with gashes of lightning which lit the sky in dramatic green and yellow flashes, she cowered in the bottom of the canoe, wishing they had something they could pull over their heads.

But for once Ward had nothing, and when the rains came they were compelled to sit tight and get soaked. It was as though they were under a giant waterfall, and the once smooth waters of the river were churned into a frothy, muddy chocolate torrent which took them along at great speed, tossing the boat from side to side like a piece of driftwood.

Verna was terrified and clung desperately to Ward. He pushed her away, saying harshly, 'Get baling, if you don't want to capsize!'

She then realised that their boat was filling with water, and frantically she grabbed a cup and scooped out as fast as she could. She was convinced they were making no progress, but they must have been, because the six inches of water in the bottom was not getting any deeper.

In a way it was a relief to have something to do. It took her mind off the terrifying storm that raged about their heads. The air was thick and dark and it was impossible to see more than a couple of yards. The banks of the river were invisible and it was as though they were in a watery world of their own.

This is it, thought Verna, as the lightning got

closer and closer, each silver flash outlined in red. We're destined for a watery grave—if the alligators don't get us first! No way could they survive in those turbulent waters.

Ward, as usual, was taking it all in his stride, baling smoothly and quickly and from all outward signs totally indifferent to the thunder and lightning that raged above their heads.

It was the worst storm Verna had ever experienced, and she hoped she would never get caught in anything like it again. It would have been enjoyable to watch from the refuge of some snug room, but out here in the middle of it she was convinced they were as close to hell as she would ever get.

And then, as dramatically as it had begun, it finished. The sky cleared, a rainbow appeared in a shimmering arc, and the river, although still swiftly flowing and at least a foot higher up the banks than it had been, became smooth and less frightening, and Verna gave Ward a weak smile.

She was deathly cold, her teeth chattering as she tried to speak. 'I didn't think we'd make it.'

'Faith,' he said. 'I never had any doubts.'

'You wouldn't!' she replied tensely. 'Doesn't anything ever frighten you?'

'Oh, I have been scared,' he admitted. 'Many times. The brave part is not to show it.'

'If you're asking me to do that,' said Verna, 'you're asking the wrong person. I was frankly terrified, and no way could I have hidden it.'

'Faced with it often enough, you'd learn,' he said confidently. 'We'll stop as soon as we can and finish our mopping-up operations.' He grinned suddenly. 'I daren't tell you what you look like!'

'I don't think I want to know,' Verna knew how she felt—that was enough.

Before long they found a sandbank that had not

been totally submerged by the swollen river, and Ward made his way towards it, Verna helping him pull the boat up so that there was no danger of it drifting away.

A search of the haversack proved that, because it was plastic-lined, everything had kept relatively dry. 'I suggest you change your clothes,' said Ward. 'They'll soon dry on you, now the sun's graced us with her presence once again, but you'll feel better for a change and a good rub down with a towel.'

Indeed she would, thought Verna. The only problem was, where? The few square yards of sand offered no protection whatsoever.

He saw her hesitation. 'Heavens!' he exclaimed. 'Don't say you're going to go coy on me after what we've been through together. Besides, I seem to recall seeing a painting of you in your London flat—in the nude?' His brows rose quizzically.

'So what?' she demanded angrily, resenting him prying. 'That was art—it was different.' Besides, David never saw her as a woman, she was convinced of that. It *had* been different. Not once had she felt embarrassed when posing for David, but in front of this man? Well—she would not feel safe.

'Mmm, how different, I wonder,' he said, his eyes alight with amusement. 'But if it will make you feel any better I'll turn my back. How's that?'

Verna did not altogether trust him, but what choice had she? Sitting in wet clothes until they dried on her? They would not take long, she knew, but she felt desperately uncomfortable and longed for a change more than anything.

Hastily she stripped off, scrubbing her damp body with the towel until it was glowing and vibrant. She pulled on a clean shirt and a pair of briefs, then realised that she had only the one pair of trousers with her.

'What am I supposed to do for trousers?' she asked sarcastically. 'It was your brainy idea that I leave all my others behind.'

Ward turned, grinning insolently, his eyes taking in the full length of her legs. 'I'll fix a line and we'll hang them up to dry. By the time we've made ourselves a drink they should be ready.'

'And how about you?' she queried crossly. 'I bet you brought a spare pair?'

'Oh no, I wouldn't do that on you, my lovely hostile lady.' And so saying he dropped his jeans and stripped off his shirt. She turned before he could pull off his underpants as well, annoyed when he chuckled deliberately.

In no time at all he had strung a line between two clumps of bamboo and their sodden clothes were steaming in the heat from the sun. He lit the Primus and soon a pan of water bubbled merrily. It did not look too appetising, as the river was still a murky brown, but once the coffee was made, Verna shut her mind to the condition of the water and sipped it gratefully.

She was hot again already, perspiration trickling down her face and back, and she could not help wondering whether she would suffer any ill effects from her soaking. Being ill in the jungle was the last thing she wanted.

Ward sprawled out at her side, his pants, already dry, clinging to him like a second skin, apparently oblivious to the sickening heat. She could almost imagine him saying. 'This is the life!'

'I'm hungry,' she said quietly.

He smiled. 'Do you know, I knew you were going to say that! But for the moment I'm afraid you'll have to put up with it.'

'Haven't you got anything?' she asked incredulously.

'It's no good eating up all our stock,' he said. 'We'll push on in a minute, and when we stop again maybe I'll shoot a wild pig or something. That will keep us going for quite a while. And we'll gather fruit, so you can satiate your seemingly perpetual hunger while we're moving. Heaven knows where you put it all—you're as thin as a rake.'

'Thanks for the compliment,' she snapped. Being hungry in no way helped her temper. 'And for your information, I'm not usually so greedy. It must be the outdoor life. Are our things dry?'

She jumped up and pulled her jeans from the improvised line. They were bone dry and as stiff as a board, and when she tried to pull them on she realised they had shrunk.

It was a struggle, and Ward grinned all the time. 'A good job you haven't eaten,' he remarked, 'or you'd never get into them.'

'Let's see what's happened to yours,' she snapped, tossing them across and standing arms akimbo while he stepped into them. Annoyingly they moulded his lean hips as perfectly as they had before.

He buttoned his shirt and tucked it in, an irritating smile on his lips. Verna looked round wildly for something to throw, even more annoyed when there was nothing.

He packed their things into the boat and looked back over his shoulder, seemingly ignorant of her anger. 'Help me push it out,' he called, 'unless you intend staying here by yourself?'

Verna threw him a black look and pushed the boat into the water. His thigh brushed hers and she shot away as though she had been bit.

Ward grinned and held out his hand. She ignored it, clambering in with what dignity she could muster. His teasing was worse than his anger.

It was difficult to ignore him, sitting so close in the narrow canoe, but she did her best, riveting her attention on the now smoothly flowing river, sometimes trailing her fingers and scooping up water to cool her overheated body.

He whistled as he paddled rhythmically, and this irritated her even more. He had no right to be so happy! Whenever she caught his eyes he smiled and she turned angrily away, aware that her bad temper was amusing him, but unable to do anything about it.

She was hungry and irritable, and her mosquito bites itched like hell, and she wished she had never set eyes on Ward Levitt. Why couldn't he have let her have some of their precious rations? Why was he so adamant about reserving them?

It suddenly struck her that perhaps he was not so confident about them getting out of this jungle as he made out. Could that be the reason? She was appalled at the thought—but it was a definite possibility.

Her horror was clearly reflected on her face, for his eyes suddenly narrowed and he said harshly, 'Now what are you thinking?'

'Why should I be thinking anything?' she parried quickly.

'Because your face is like an open book. You looked suddenly frightened to death.'

'Did I?' She wished she had been more careful. She did not want to admit her fears. He would only laugh and assure her that they were unfounded—but that might not necessarily be true. He could well be lying for her benefit, knowing how terrified she was already.

'Oh, hell, Verna, stop dallying!' His good humour had gone. 'Something's troubling you—what is it?'

She shrugged and said fatalistically, 'I had a sudden horrifying premonition that we're never going to get out of here alive.'

'Is that all?' he asked lightly. 'You've been thinking that all along.'

'I can't help it,' she snapped. 'I've never been in a predicament like this before. How do I know that you're not simply pretending we'll be rescued, that you know there's no hope, but you're not admitting it for fear of frightening me?'

He slapped a hand impatiently to his brow. 'You couldn't be much more alarmed than you already are. Take my word for it, I'm not keeping anything back. We shall get out of here—and alive.'

'Then why wouldn't you let me have anything to eat?' she demanded crossly.

He suddenly laughed. 'So that's it! You're still annoyed with me for refusing you food?'

'Not just for refusing,' she said, even more incensed by his amusement. 'Your reason for doing it.'

'And what's that supposed to mean? Didn't I make myself clear?'

'Oh, very,' she cried. 'We can't eat because we don't know how long we'll be stuck in this place. I reckon it'll be for a darn sight longer than you're letting on. I reckon you even have your doubts that we'll make it at all.'

He looked at her long and hard before he finally spoke. 'Have I ever lied to you, Verna?' he asked smoothly, grimly.

She lifted her shoulders expressively. 'You could have done—how would I know, unless I catch you out?'

'Do I look like a man who lies?' he demanded.

She pulled a face. 'Not really, but——'

'But nothing,' he snarled. 'You're spoiling for a

fight, aren't you? Haven't you the common sense to realise that we're in a bad enough position as it is, without constantly bickering?'

'There, I knew something was wrong!' cried Verna, tears springing to the back of her eyes. 'We are in more trouble than you're letting on. Why don't you admit it? Why do you keep trying to fob me off with your ridiculous lies?'

'Be quiet, Verna,' he said tightly. 'You're becoming hysterical.'

She glared, her green eyes twin pools of fire. 'I am not! I am never hysterical.'

'You've never been in a situation like this before,' he returned with amazing calmness. 'It's easy to overreact.'

'And it's easy for you to say that everything will be all right. I just wish I had your faith!' and she collapsed in the bottom of the boat, her tears falling freely now.

She heard him swear softly, but he made no attempt to console her. He merely carried on propelling their vessel, ignoring her outburst—which merely made her all the more resentful.

Long after she had finished crying she kept her head buried, maintaining a huffy silence and wishing him a thousand miles away. Even when she sensed he had stopped paddling and there was movement in the canoe she did not look up. It was up to him to make the first approach.

But the sound of a gunshot, very close to her ear, made her shriek out in terror, and she stood up so quickly that for a moment there was a real danger of her toppling over into the river.

Ward steadied her impatiently. 'What the hell did you do that for?'

'Why were you shooting?' she demanded. 'You frightened me to death!'

He pointed to the far sandbank. 'Wild boar,' he said succinctly. 'I was lucky. A whole herd must have crossed the river just before we approached. I caught sight of the last one and managed to get him. At least you needn't go hungry now.'

Deep footprints in the sand told her that there had indeed been a whole lot of animals at this point. The one Ward had shot lay limp and lifeless, and she could not help feeling sorry that they had had to destroy a live animal merely to subsist themselves.

But her hunger was greater than her pity, and when Ward steered towards the shore she was as eager as he to get the animal cooked.

They found a gap in the undergrowth where the boar had crashed through, and Ward cleared away a small area so that he could build a fire. Verna gathered wood and helped as much as she could, but she was compelled to turn her back as he cut the animal into manageable pieces.

Soon, however, a delicious smell of roasting pig permeated the air, and crisp, golden joints cooked above the fire on Ward's improvised barbecue. On another fire Verna cooked rice and boiled water, and her salivary glands were working overtime.

The meal was as tasty as she had expected. The wild pig was sweet and tender and flavoured with woodsmoke, and she ate as much as she liked.

Ward too looked more complacent by the time they had finished. 'That was good,' he said, wiping his fingers on the seat of his pants. 'You look better too. Did you enjoy it?'

She nodded. 'Though if anyone had asked me a week ago if I fancied eating wild pig I'd have emphatically denied it.'

'Mm,' he said. 'It's surprising what you eat when your life depends on it.' He finished cooking the rest of the meat, then packed it carefully into the bottom of the boat. 'If my calculations are correct,' he told her, 'we have about another hour's travelling, then we must leave the boat behind and make the rest of the way on foot. I'd like to do the river bit before nightfall. Are you game?'

Verna nodded and smiled. She felt fit for anything at this very moment, though she was not so sure she would feel this way for long once they were tramping through the jungle. Who knew what hidden dangers awaited them?

The sun had begun to set again when they finally reached the spot Ward was looking for. It was another of those fantastic sunsets when the sky was streaked with vermilion and gold and the sun looked like a huge ball of fire sinking rapidly below the horizon.

Ward set up their camp and managed to get a fire going before darkness fell. He slung their hammocks and they sat talking, for once in complete harmony.

Verna discovered that he owned a shipping company with offices in both Manaus and Belém, as well as others in different parts of the world. But he preferred to live in Brazil. 'It's terrifically hot and humid and not everyone can stand it, especially Europeans,' he said pointedly. 'But it suits me—and Guy too. He loves it. I once asked him if he ever fancied returning to England—but he said no. He's quite happy here, and I guess this is where he'll spend the rest of his days.'

'What does he do?' she asked.

Ward affected surprise. 'At last the lady shows interest! He's retired, has been for the last few years. I bought him out, as a matter of fact.'

And he had once worked *for* Guy Pemberton! Talk about climbing to the top of the tree! 'You must be a very rich man,' she remarked.

'I suppose so,' he admitted, 'though I don't count my happiness in personal wealth.'

'Are you married?' she asked next, surprising herself at her outspoken question.

'Do I look married?' he parried lightly. 'No, as a matter of fact, I'm not, though I'm not disputing that there've been plenty of girls who would have liked to be Mrs Ward Levitt. I value my freedom too much, I think. I've never fancied tying myself down.'

'I don't think marriage does that,' she said sharply. 'If you're in love it's surely a pleasure to be with the one you love, not a trap—as you seem to suggest?'

He shrugged easily. 'As I've never been married I wouldn't know. Are you an expert on these matters? Have you ever contemplated getting married yourself?'

Verna shook her head emphatically. 'No! I don't intend to ever get married. My mother's disastrous affair was enough to put me off the idea for life.'

'She laid down the poison?' he hinted. 'What exactly did she tell you about your father? I understood you to say that she told you he was dead?'

'You're a rat,' she snapped. 'You really have it in for my mother, don't you? But to get the facts right, she did tell me he was dead. That was a long time ago—when I was about six. I never asked her about him again.'

Ward frowned, the planes of his face harshly angular in the light from the fire. 'I find that puzzling. It's unnatural that you should show so little interest.'

'I suppose she discouraged me from talking about him,' she admitted. 'My mother didn't like men at all. As a matter of fact she warned me off them—and meeting you, I can see why.'

'I don't follow your reasoning.' He swung his legs over the side of the hammock, watching her closely through narrowed eyes. 'I've not forced my attentions upon you. In no way have I made myself objectionable. My only sin was an oil leak in the plane—something entirely out of my control.'

She did not like to admit that he was right. 'You did kiss me once,' she cried wildly, 'and if I hadn't made it quite clear that I object to that sort of thing I've no doubt you would have tried it on again.'

'That's what your mother told you—that men only see women as sex objects?'

She nodded. 'Isn't it true? Apart from David, I've never found that any of you are any different.'

'Hence the cold front?' he queried, his lips quirking with annoying amusement. 'And who's the lucky David, I wonder? Your artist friend?'

'As a matter of fact, yes,' she spat. 'Not that I consider it any of your business.'

He swung down from his hammock and walked slowly over to her. 'You're right, it's not, and I shan't mention him again.'

'Good,' she said icily, eyeing him warily as he approached her hammock. He stood in front of her, arms folded across his powerful chest, an enigmatic smile on his face. 'What do you want now?' she demanded crossly. 'Isn't it time we were considering getting ready for sleep?'

Electric impulses leapt from him to her and she strove desperately to ignore them. Alarm flared in her eyes and he laughed softly. 'Worried, are you, that I'm about to live up to the reputation your mother unkindly unloaded on to all us unfortunate men?'

'I wouldn't put it past you,' she flashed. 'We've

been together for four days now. For all I know you may be feeling frustrated.'

His eyes hardened. 'And I'd need to be a whole lot more frustrated before I'd work it out on you!'

She gasped. 'I don't think that was called for, Ward Levitt. I suggest you apologise immediately.'

'Why should I?' he asked, his eyes wide and protesting. 'You make it quite clear you don't want me to touch you. Besides, I like my women warm and passionate, not cold little fish who don't know their own mind.'

'Oh, I hate you!' she cried, resenting his implication.

'So you keep telling me. Are you sure it's not yourself you're trying to convince?'

She wished he would move away. His nearness disturbed her even though she was reluctant to admit it. 'I know my own feelings,' she replied passionately. 'And so far as you're concerned it's hate with a capital H.'

'In that case,' he said grimly, 'I'm sorry you've had my company forced upon you. Rest assured that I shall do my utmost not to increase your hatred. It's not very pleasant to find oneself the object of so much venom.'

Verna suddenly wished she had not spoken so unkindly. She did not really hate him—not that much anyway. He irritated her more than anything. He was so complacent, so very much in control, and so damned sexually attractive!

This was the really annoying part. She did not want to become tempted by him, yet it would be so easy! Stuck as they were with each other's company for every hour of every day, nothing could be more natural than that they should turn to each other.

Yet Ward had shown not the remotest interest,

and she was certainly not going to give him any encouragement. She had no intention of being used—for the sake of sex alone. Her mother's doctrine had been well and truly drilled into her.

'Help me down,' she said testily. 'I need a walk before turning in for the night.'

He obeyed, handling her carefully so that she could have no cause for complaint. He handed her his torch. 'Mind where you go, don't wander too far. And shuffle your feet in the grass, there are likely to be snakes. They won't bite unless trodden on, and if they hear you coming they'll move away.'

'Are you trying to deter me from going?' Her voice was strongly angry.

'Hell, no. The farther the better is how I feel right at this moment. But unfortunately I do feel concerned for your safety, so please, no heroics. Keep within calling distance.'

She was afraid to go anywhere after that, but the call of nature was stronger. She stamped in the long grass with exaggerated caution. She had no doubt that Ward had not simply been trying to frighten her. He seemed to know a great deal about these things.

She was back within minutes to find that Ward had fixed her mosquito net and banked the fire. He was already in his own hammock. She called, 'Goodnight,' but he did not answer. She gave a mental shrug, surprisingly hurt, and climbed into bed.

It was no mean feat, working her way into the hammock without letting the mosquitoes inside the net, but eventually she made it, although she had no sooner settled than she heard the distinct drone of one of them who must have escaped her vigilant eye. He landed on her face, the only piece of bare skin available, and she slapped at the same time as she felt his bite.

She scratched and itched the whole night through, marvelling that her companion could lie so still and sleep so deeply. Did nothing bother him?

He was so disgustingly fit and healthy; it was annoying. She could not remember seeing him with one bite, whereas she herself was literally covered from head to toe—great red bumps that itched and irritated until they almost drove her out of her mind.

## CHAPTER SIX

THE going was hard the next day. Verna had not realised how easy the canoe had made things for them. At times there was a track of sorts to follow, but at others Ward ploughed off into the jungle, hacking a passage with his knife, she following blindly.

He seemed to know exactly which direction to take, and the fact that he had the heavy haversack on his back did not hamper him at all.

By the end of the first hour Verna was ready to drop. 'I'll have to rest,' she said, sinking down, then jumping up again hastily to discover she had sat on an army of ants.

Desperately she knocked them from her, and then screamed as a hairy centipede nearly eight inches long fell on her arm from the trees above.

'Don't touch it!' yelled Ward at once. 'The hairs are poisonous.'

He found a twig and flicked the alarming insect away, and Verna felt almost faint with fright and exhaustion. 'I must sit down,' she cried. 'I can't go on any longer.'

She expected irritation, was pleasantly surprised when he said, 'But of course, I'd forgotten you're not used to this sort of thing. You're doing very well, considering. I can allow you no more than a few minutes, though. We must press on.'

He found a dead tree trunk, inspected it for possible poisonous insects, then said, 'Sit here. I noticed a few guava trees a little way back—I'll go and pick some. They might make you feel better.'

Verna did not want him to leave her, but wisely said nothing, all the time looking about her with wide apprehensive eyes. She did not fancy being jumped on by some wild animal. She even went so far as to take the gun from her bag, though she knew she would be too shaky to use it.

Ward laughed when he returned. 'I wouldn't have left you if I hadn't thought you'd be quite safe. Put that thing away before it scares you to death. You're holding it as though it's going to bite you!'

The guavas, which she discovered were a type of plum, were succulent and delicious, some of them a yellow pink with sweet red pips, others green and firmer with a slightly acid taste which Verna found more satisfying.

'Put the rest in your bag,' said Ward, when she had eaten her fill. 'They should keep you going until lunchtime.'

Again he forged on, but this time his pace was somewhat slower, and Verna found herself more able to keep up—and the guavas helped too, quenching her seemingly perpetual thirst.

Sometimes the track opened out so that they could see the blue sky. Occasional vultures circled, making her shudder. It was almost as though they were waiting for her to succumb. She quickened her steps to catch up with Ward. The man had an inexhaustible supply of energy, only the slightest film of perspiration covered his brow, though she did notice that his shirt clung wetly to his magnificent body.

Some of the plants they passed were dangerous, because of thorns and poisonous barbs. But in compensation there were thick clumps of bamboo as high as a house, and all sorts of exotic flowers in brilliant reds and blues. Multi-coloured butterflies as big as her hand flitted in front of her, and the birds' chorus was like nothing she had ever heard.

Frequently blue, red and yellow macaws flew through the trees in splendid splashes of colour, frogs croaked, and it was all so incredibly beautiful that it was easy to forget the jungle's hidden dangers.

Long before lunchtime Verna began to feel the strain and her steps became slower and slower, despite, a determined effort to maintain the pace. 'I'll have to rest again,' she called.

But this time he was not so tolerant. 'Another couple of miles and we'll stop for lunch,' he said briskly. 'Surely you can manage that?'

His impatience goaded her into a positive, 'But of course. It was foolish of me to suggest stopping. I'm so sorry.'

Her sarcasm was not lost on him, but still he did not stop, and Verna was compelled to stumble in his wake. Although cooler beneath the trees the air was still thick and choking and the perspiration ran down her as though she had stepped from a shower.

By sheer determination she made the last mile. They had come upon a reasonable track and the going was much easier than when they were chopping their way through tough fibrous plants and grasses.

She was furious with Ward, as well as being so desperately weak and tired that she felt she was going to die, and when he eventually called a halt, she could not help saying, 'Are you sure you want to stop? Wouldn't you like to go on another few miles—kill me off altogether?'

He frowned harshly. 'You've managed, what are you complaining about?'

'I've managed!' she mocked, rolling her eyes skywards. 'But only just. I hope you don't intend going any farther today, because if you do you'll have to carry me.'

'You'll do it,' he said tightly. 'It's surprising what you can do if you have to.'

'But that's just it! We don't *have* to.' What an uncompassionate man he was. 'I'm not one of your Amazon women, I'm a town-bred office worker, and if you don't want a corpse on your hands you'd better remember that!'

'Sit down,' he said impatiently. 'I'll fix our lunch.'

Verna checked carefully for an area free from insects. The middle of the track seemed to be best, so regardless that the dirt would probably turn to mud when mixed with the sweat on her body she threw herself down, stretching out full length, and felt the tension gradually ease out of her tired muscles.

Overhead, the canopy of green let in shafts of golden sunlight, dappling the surrounding area in a motley of yellow-green hues. One ray of sunshine illuminated to perfection a beautiful spray of orchid with flowers more enormous than any she had ever seen—vivid purple streaked with brilliant pink in a confusion of colour that almost hurt the eyes.

Everything in the jungle seemed to be bigger and better than anything that grew elsewhere. If they weren't so isolated, so completely cut off from the rest of civilisation, she would have been enchanted with her surroundings.

As it was, she admired its beauty, but wished herself anywhere but in that precise spot. She was afraid to ask Ward how far off he thought they were from the post he had mentioned. Better to be ignorant, she decided, than be faced with the stark facts of what could still be a frightening and exhausting journey.

She closed her eyes for a while. She felt as though she was sinking into the ground and everything began to spin. Then she was dreaming that she was being chased by a jaguar. She ran and ran, screaming for Ward.

With her lungs bursting she tripped and fell, and watched in horror as the yellow spotted beast sprang. Within inches, it seemed, of him ravaging her, a shot rang out. With an angry snarl he turned, then died an instant death, falling crushingly across her legs.

She was woken by Ward shaking her shoulder and her screams echoing in the trees. 'Wake up!' he said sharply.

Verna sat abruptly, her eyes wide and panic-struck. 'The jaguar!' she cried. 'You shot him?'

'You were dreaming.' His voice was sharp, as though he thought she had no right to fall asleep. 'Here, drink this,' and he thrust a mug of black coffee into her hand.

Gratefully she sipped it, the strong liquid reviving, so that she could almost forget it had all been a dream. 'Are there jaguars in these parts?' she asked, a frown creasing her forehead.

He nodded, reluctantly, she thought. 'But so long as you don't go wandering off on your own you'll be all right.'

He needn't have warned her. No way was she likely to do that. Her dream had been vivid enough to make her realise the perils of leaving this dependable man. He was her life-saver, whether she liked it or not.

They ate chunks of wild pig and the remainder of the flat cakes of manioc bread given to them by the Indians. For dessert Verna ate two more of her guavas and drank another cup of coffee, and after that she began to feel better.

Her limbs still ached intolerably, though, and she did not feel in the least like moving on. A blister had formed on both heels and she took off her shoes, searching in the haversack for the first aid box.

Ward said peremptorily, 'Let me. Why didn't you mention these earlier? It must have been hell to walk with your feet in this condition.'

'Would you have stopped?' she asked faintly. 'I doubt it, you'd have thought I was making excuses.'

'I'm not totally insensitive to your condition,' he returned bitterly.

'You could have fooled me,' she muttered, wincing as he pressed the plasters to her feet.

His lips thinned, but he said nothing, delving into the bag again and reaching out a pair of his own thick socks. 'Try these, they might help.'

'Thanks,' she said ungraciously, wondering why he couldn't have come up with them before. They would have certainly offered more protection than her nylon tights. 'I'm obviously not such a good Boy Scout as you, I didn't come adequately prepared. Why didn't you warn me there was a possibility of a holiday in the jungle?'

His blue eyes were dangerously angry, but he controlled his temper admirably. 'As soon as you're ready we'll move on.' Deftly he packed their plates and cups and then stood waiting while she laced her shoes.

She stood with difficulty, feeling irritated when he made no offer to help.

For a further hour Verna struggled on, conscious that not once had Ward looked back to see whether she was all right. She could have dropped dead right in the middle of the track and he would not have noticed, she thought angrily.

So much for his declaration that he knew exactly how she felt! If he did he would not insist on keeping this ridiculous pace. It was all right for him, he was a man—and a superbly fit one at that.

She guessed the temperature must be about a hundred degrees and constantly she wiped the sweat from her brow on the sleeve of her shirt. She hated to think what she looked like. She had refrained from looking in her handbag mirror ever since they began this hazardous journey. Oh, for the luxury of a bath!

When once more Ward veered off through the jungle and their passage became even more difficult she felt close to tears. She had sworn to herself that she would not give in, that she would show Ward Levitt that she was made of strong stuff, but unbidden came the prick of tears and she knew she could not last out much longer.

Her soaking jeans rubbed her legs as she walked and the strap of her handbag cut into her shoulder. She found it difficult to breathe in this cloying heat and even the guavas could no longer assuage her thirst.

As they picked their way over tangled roots, pushing back clawing branches, and avoiding needle-sharp thorns, she felt very close to breaking down altogether, begging Ward to stop, pleading with him even.

And when her foot caught in a hidden root and she pitched headlong on to her face she burst into uncontrollable tears, lying there sobbing, cursing fate for throwing her to the mercy of this man.

Instantly he was at her side, gravely solicitous, helping her sit, cradling her in his strong, muscular arms. 'It's my fault,' he said, 'I was pushing you too hard.'

And because he was concerned, because he was apologising, Verna felt even worse, and her shoulders shook as she sobbed helplessly against his chest.

'I'm sorry,' she mumbled at length, sniffing indelicately, and accepting the rather less than clean handkerchief he held out. She blew her nose and mopped her eyes, and felt better.

'Poor little Verna!' He was smiling suddenly and tracing a finger down her nose. 'You look a sight, do you know that? All red and sunburnt and streaked with mud, and your lovely blonde curls tangled and dark with perspiration.'

'You don't exactly look like an advert for the best-dressed man yourself,' she returned huffily.

He grinned and squeezed her gently. 'I'm only kidding. You look wonderful. You've amazed me, with your stamina and your courage. I've known men who'd have called it a day long before now.'

She smiled weakly, looking up into the powerful blue of his eyes. There was something comforting about being held in his arms in this wild primitive place and it made her heartbeats quicken with unwarranted urgency.

Gently he brushed her lips with his own, and incongruously from somewhere in the trees overhead a bird trilled out a wolf whistle. 'He's jealous,' said Ward softly, increasing the pressure of his lips when he found no resistance.

Verna could not have fought anyway, she had not the strength. And strangely she was content to let him kiss her, finding satisfaction in their physical contact.

Previously, it was as though she had been alone in the jungle. Ward had stalked on ahead, ignoring her almost, and certainly not offering any words of comfort or encouragement.

A helping hand was all she had desired, not his stony silence and the knowledge that she would blindly follow at whatever personal cost. Now that was changed.

She sensed restrained passion behind his carefully controlled kisses and knew that the onus lay on her. The slightest encouragement and his love-making would take on a new meaning. At the moment they were kisses of comfort.

The question to ask herself was whether she wanted his caresses. He had accused her of being cold, but she knew from that other time he had kissed her that he was capable of evoking deep fires.

'My silly, sweet Verna,' he said softly, his lips trailing to the delicate area behind her ears. 'Why didn't you stop me? I'm a thoughtless fool, I was concerned only with reaching a certain spot before nightfall.'

Her eyes widened in alarm. 'Do we still have to go on?'

He shook his head, smiling tenderly. 'We'll make camp here. It will do us both good to rest, then maybe tomorrow we'll be able to——'

'There you go again!' she accused. 'I don't care how long it takes so long as we don't have to keep up this gruelling pace. The weight's dropping off me! I'll be nothing more than a living skeleton by the time we get to Belém.'

He looked at her carefully. 'Maybe you are a little thinner, but that's only natural in this heat. You'll soon put it on again. Guy will see to that, I'm sure.'

It was funny, she had almost forgotten the reason they were here. Now her thoughts turned to the man who claimed to be her father. 'Do you think he's worried?'

'I should think he's half out of his mind,' said Ward firmly. 'But there's nothing we can do about it. We have ourselves to consider at the moment.' So saying he ravaged her mouth again and this time Verna clung to him desperately, unable to contain her own feelings.

When he lay down in the undergrowth, pulling her alongside him, she submitted weakly, aware of a genuine pleasure at the touch of his body against her own.

They were both burning up with the intense claustrophobic heat of the jungle, but it was as though it served to increase her desire. Verna found herself consumed with a wild animal hunger and her lips parted beneath his, her body arching involuntarily towards him.

He groaned and pulled her closer, his hands feverishly exploring. Verna forgot she was exhausted, forgot they were lying on an uncomfortable bed of thickly interwoven roots where snakes could lurk or an army of red ants bite at any minute, and gave herself up to the rapture of Ward's infinitely sweet kisses.

He plundered her mouth as no man ever had, making her heady with the excitement of it all. She slid her hands behind his head and clung to him desperately.

She was intoxicated by the male smell of him and when he stopped kissing her she kissed him, covering his face, moving her body sensually against him, vividly aware of his arousal and knowing that she was treading on dangerous ground.

She was encouraging Ward, shamelessly, but it was as though something inside her had taken over, and there was nothing she could do to stop herself.

And then suddenly a prickle ran down her spine. Ward was looking behind her. His hands had stilled and there was a faintly wary expression on his face.

Slowly she turned her head, expecting to see some wild animal posed for attack, at the very least a ten-foot snake hanging from a tree. What she was not prepared for was the fierce-looking Indian standing over them, and an involuntary cry of alarm rose in her throat.

She clutched Ward, her green eyes wide and troubled.

'It's all right,' he said. 'He's merely curious.'

'I hope you're right,' she whispered, struggling to her feet, but still clinging to Ward's arm for comfort.

The man was tall, wide-shouldered and powerful, his brown body gleaming like polished wood. His arms and legs were tightly bound with bands of palm, he wore a string of beads round his waist and larger white beads hung from his ears. His long hair was tied back in a knot.

The bow and arrow in his hand seemed threatening and Verna clung desperately to her companion, her heart thudding painfully from sheer terror, in contrast to the raw emotion that had filled her before.

Ward said a few words in Portuguese and although it was apparent that their visitor had not understood all he said, he had recognised enough to get the gist of things.

He beckoned for them to follow, a slow smile revealing even white teeth, and when she looked closer Verna saw that his oval brown eyes were twinkling. It had clearly amused him, catching them in such an uncompromising situation. She expected it was the most unlikely sight he was ever likely to see in his jungle.

He marched ahead at a pace that even outdid Ward and she was compelled to run and stumble to keep up with his galloping stride. But with Ward's helping hand she did not mind—all she could do was wonder where they were going, and be thankful that the Indian was friendly.

It came as a complete surprise when they stepped out of the jungle into a clearing that had certainly not been apparent until they were right on top of it.

The huts were rectangular with walls made from wooden poles and roofs of plaited palm fronds. Vines hung with giant gourds climbed up the walls and nearby were guava trees and the sweet scent of lime, and it all looked very orderly.

A group of Indians stood watching them, silent and unsmiling in their appraisal, but as soon as it became apparent that the intruders were friendly they all began talking at once, the women crowding round Verna, touching her hair bleached almost white now by the sun.

The Indians looked different from the other tribe they had seen. The women were a much lighter honey colour, slim and straight with skins as smooth as satin. The men were more finely built with short straight hair and a definite European look about their features.

They welcomed Verna and Ward quite overwhelmingly, taking them into their huts and proudly showing their possessions. Verna was given a gift of a comb made from pine needles bound with coloured threads, and she was sorry she had nothing to give in return. If only Ward had not insisted that they travel light! But he found another packet of cigarettes and handed them round and they seemed quite happy.

In mime language she asked if there was anywhere she could wash and was immediately dragged by a laughing group of young women along a narrow track where low branches curled over their heads and thick creepers hung like ropes.

To her amazement the inviting waters of a lagoon suddenly opened out in front of them. Verna could not believe her eyes, and laughing like a child she stripped off her clothes and sank into the welcome coolness of the water.

After two days without a proper wash it was heaven. She had been in for no more than a few seconds when Ward appeared, tossing her a bar of soap before he too stripped and waded into the tantalisingly clear water.

'Watch out for sting-rays on the bottom,' he warned, 'and you might see the odd water snake!' There was a wicked gleam in his eyes.

But even this did not spoil Verna's enjoyment. She soaped herself liberally, using it to wash her hair as well, not in the least disturbed that she and Ward were naked in the water.

She was too desperate for embarrassment. She had never been so hot and dirty and sticky in all her life, and no way was she going to forgo the pleasure of this moment for the sake of modesty.

'Isn't it glorious?' she called to Ward. 'My tiredness is simply melting away!'

'Good,' he quipped. 'I was afraid we might have to rest tomorrow. Now we can press on.'

'Oh, no!' she cried. 'Let's stay here. It's so beautiful, and the people are so friendly.'

His eyes crinkled. 'Like a holiday camp, in fact.'

She splashed water into his face. 'You can't

mock me, I won't let you. I feel quite happy at this moment, and you or no one is going to spoil it.'

He dived swiftly and cleanly beneath the water and the next second Verna felt her legs being pulled downwards. Her shriek was cut off as she went below the surface and there followed a playful fight as she struggled to escape his embrace.

But he intended to have his own way, and his body was like molten metal against her own, his strength undeniable as he entwined his legs about hers, his hands sliding over the curve of her breasts and hips.

He kissed her below the water and they surfaced to an interested audience. The women who had brought Verna to this enchanting place had been joined by a group of young men who quite clearly found their antics highly entertaining.

Suddenly with a whoop and a cry the water became full of naked bodies, and for the next half hour Ward and his new playmates took part in energetic games.

He had brought a couple of towels down to the lagoon with him, so Verna washed out her jeans and shirt, and bra and pants, knowing they would dry in minutes in the heat of this Brazilian sun, and then sat with a towel wrapped round her watching the activities of the men.

She no longer felt so desperately tired, and Ward had not been so far wrong when he jokingly suggested that she felt she was on holiday. With the brown-skinned friendly people, and this exotic lagoon where she could wash away her aches and pains, it was almost like paradise.

Until she remembered that they were desperately trying to fight their way out of this place! She preferred not to dwell on that. Her philosophy at this moment was to take each day as it came and not worry too much about the future.

She relied on Ward implicitly and knew that her faith would in no way be unjustified. If he could get them out of here he would.

Watching him now as he entered races with the athletic Indians, she realised he kept up with the best of them and very often won. They seemed delighted with his company and had no difficulty in understanding his Portuguese.

Verna wondered what would have happened had they not been interrupted by the powerful Indian earlier. She was almost afraid to analyse her feelings so far as Ward was concerned. They were slowly and inexorably undergoing a change. He was getting beneath her skin whether she liked it or not.

Even looking at him now sent her pulses racing, and impatiently she jumped up, deciding to go for a walk along the shore of the lake. The sand was burning hot to the soles of her feet and she stepped carefully, keeping a wary eye open for snakes.

Green and yellow parakeets flew overhead, sometimes alighting on the path before her, their voices loud and cackling, another bird trilled happily somewhere unseen, butterflies landed on her shoulders, and she felt ridiculously happy.

It was stupid really. Here she was cut off from civilisation, not knowing when their traumatic journey was going to end, indeed if it did end—and she was happy!

She dared not admit that her new feelings for Ward Levitt had anything to do with it. He was a tough uncaring man, and circumstances had forced them together. As he had said a few days earlier, people behaved differently in the jungle, their sense of values changed. Once back in civilisation she would undoubtedly see him in an entirely different light—and he would certainly have no interest in her. He had made that very clear.

When she returned she realised that she had been so engrossed in her thoughts that she had not noticed the men had finished their swimming. The Indians had returned to their village and Ward lay full length on the sand, watching her lazily through narrowed eyes, clad only in a brief pair of brilliantly patterned underpants, his shirt and jeans hung over a bush to dry beside her own.

In the light of her newly discovered feelings, Verna felt hesitant to face him, grabbing her clothes and looking for somewhere to dress safe from his probing gaze.

But he caught her ankle and pulled her down. 'You're not running away?' he suggested mockingly. 'We have unfinished business—remember? And I think we're both feeling a whole lot fresher now.'

'I can't recall any—unfinished business,' she said haughtily. 'Please let go, Ward, you're hurting.'

He released her ankle, but his arm came heavily across her waist, imprisoning her at his side. There was a scornful lift to his brows. 'The original ice maiden returns, is that it?'

'If you mean do I still want you to kiss me, then the answer is no.'

'And why the sudden change of heart?'

'It's not that,' she returned stoutly. 'I was upset, you were comforting me, that's all. And now I no longer need you.'

'But I want you.' His voice was raw with emotion, his blue eyes dark with desire.

Verna felt herself begin to tremble and desperately tried to break free. No good could come from giving herself to Ward like this. She had never involved herself in casual affairs, and now was certainly not the time to start.

'Don't fight,' he said softly. 'Relax, I'm not going to hurt you.'

'I'm not afraid of getting hurt,' she snapped.

'But of making a fool of yourself, perhaps? Ruining the carefully contrived image you've developed?'

She eyed him coldly. 'I wasn't aware that I had.'

'Oh yes,' he smiled, 'but it has weakened once or twice recently—and I think with a little practice you could shed it altogether.'

Verna tossed her head angrily. 'I don't know what you're talking about.'

'I think you do.' His smile was slow and warm, his hand on her nape, fingers caressing.

When his mouth sought hers a flame leapt between them. He cupped her face with both hands, kissing her deeply, invading the moist warmth of her mouth.

For a few seconds she struggled, that was all. An ache in the pit of her stomach slowly spread, filling her body with a consuming fire which drugged her senses and made her arch herself against him.

She closed her eyes and gave herself up to the ecstasy of the moment, knowing that to fight would be futile. And did she really want to?

Her body instinctively responded to this man, he was like a drug, one taste and she was hooked, and she could not deny that the experience was a pleasurable one.

A soft moan escaped her as a sensual need of him welled up, and he groaned and pulled her on top of him, whipping away the towel in one swift fluid movement.

Her breasts were crushed against his hair-roughened chest. A new urgency developed in his kisses and Verna heard alarm bells in her head.

But she ignored them, her need as great as his own.

'Verna,' he mouthed, his kisses burning a trail to the soft hollow of her throat. 'Oh, God, I want you!'

His hands slid over her quivering body, intimately possessive, staking his claim, pressing her hips against him, emphasising his own desperate need.

Verna was torn, her own ravaging hunger fighting the warning note in her mind. She half lifted herself from him, her green eyes soft and pleading, willing him to understand.

There was agony on his face as he rolled over, his leg forcing her thighs apart.

'No, Ward,' she begged, as he began kissing her breasts, gently biting, turning her limbs to water and causing her heart to pound painfully inside her.

'No, what?' he jerked, intense blue eyes raking her face. 'You want this as much as me. Deny it if you can.'

She shook her head wildly. 'It's all wrong, Ward, I can't——'

He silenced her with a kiss and the scorching heat from his body seared into her, adding fuel to the flames that consumed her.

'How can it be wrong,' he argued, 'when we both need each other?' His body was tense, his weight pressing her into the sand. Above, the powerful sun beat down on them, and Verna knew that the outcome of all this lay in her own hands.

Quite suddenly her mind cleared. 'Because I don't love you,' she protested. 'I'm an old-fashioned girl. I happen to believe that two people should be married before they make love.' And she prayed that he would believe her, because she knew that she could not hold out much longer.

She had never desired a man as she did Ward, but she also realised that once out of this place she would regret giving in to him. It was a moment of jungle madness, that was all. Circumstances had thrust them together and just because Ward, like most other men she had met, wanted her, there was no need for her to be equally foolish.

Ward's face worked violently and Verna wondered in a sudden breathless moment whether he would take her despite what she had said. Then with an angry gesture he pushed himself up, his face grim and forbidding.

For a few long seconds he stood looking down, his powerful body taut, his lips clamped angrily. His eyes slid over the soft roundness of her breasts, the smooth flatness of her stomach, and Verna drew a shuddering breath, conscious of an unbearable ache in her lower limbs.

With a strangled cry she rolled over on to her side, burying her face in her hands, and when she looked up again he had gone.

## CHAPTER SEVEN

VERNA struggled with an emotion more powerful than anything else she had ever felt, eventually getting up and with an angry self-deprecating gesture flinging herself once more into the limpid waters of the lagoon.

She swam until a chill struck her bones, then dragged herself out and got dressed. Slowly she made her way back to the camp, reluctant to face Ward, afraid that his anger might be more than she could bear.

But when she arrived she discovered a meal had been cooked in their honour and she was pulled into the centre of the laughing Indians. Ward was already there.

She glanced at him, but he was engrossed in conversation with the fierce warlike Indian who had discovered them, so she concentrated her attention instead on the delicious smells that were wafting her way.

Fish, caught in the lagoon, had been baked over the fire. The skin was crisp and brown, the inside firm and white, tasting of woodsmoke, as had the wild boar. But it was delicious and Verna ate hungrily, wiping her plate clean with flat cakes of corn meal.

There were bananas and guavas to follow, as many as she could eat, and she made a pig of herself, knowing that once they got going she would not know where her next meal was coming from.

Ward had virtually ignored her all this time, talking to the Indian as though he was an old friend, Verna not understanding one word of their Brazilian Portuguese.

Afterwards, they were shown to the hut where they would sleep the night, and Verna wished the Indians had not taken it for granted that she and Ward wanted to share the same room. The way she felt at this moment she would have preferred to share with one of the Indian women rather than Ward.

She did not trust her own feelings, and some of her apprehension must have shown on her face, because he said tersely, 'It's all right, you'll be quite safe. You made your point very clear.'

'I didn't mean to upset you,' she said hesitantly, knowing how intolerable things would be with this tension between them.

'I'm not upset,' he said strongly.

Unable to control her temper, Verna flared, 'You could have fooled me! It's going to be one hell of a journey with you in this mood!'

He sighed impatiently. 'You have only yourself to blame. I suppose I was an idiot to expect anything different from you.'

She blanched, but stood her ground. 'And I suppose I shouldn't have expected you to treat me differently either? You're like all men, after only one thing. My mother was right!' and she burst into tears.

'My God, we're not back to that again!' His voice was savage. 'I really did think that things were getting better between us.'

'If they're not, it's your fault,' she cried furiously, wiping her tears with the back of her hand, her green eyes hurt and luminous. 'Why can't you leave me alone?'

'I could say it's because you're a very beautiful young lady,' he said, 'but as you quite clearly wouldn't believe me, I won't bother. You have it firmly fixed in your mind that my motives are entirely dishonourable—so be it.' He shrugged and left the hut, and Verna stared after him.

What was he trying to say, that he found her attractive? That he was not purely dallying with her because there was no one else around? She laughed softly to herself. She would be an idiot to believe that.

She looked at their two hammocks strung side by side and wondered how she would get through the night in such close proximity. Perhaps if she could fall asleep first?

She climbed in and secured the mosquito net carefully. She was becoming used to the hammocks now and no longer found it a gymnastic feat to haul herself inside.

But although she closed her eyes and willed herself to sleep she found it impossible. Her mind was too active—and outside could be heard laughter from the Indians and occasionally Ward's voice. He was getting on very well with this tribe.

A slight breeze rustled the palm leaves and through them Verna could see the black night sky generously scattered with stars and a pendulous moon which sent beams of light slanting into their hut.

The sweet-scented lime leaves and the lingering odour of fish pervaded the air. The hammock was coarse and scratchy and Verna knew she would not sleep.

She slid to her feet and made her way outside, standing for a silent moment surveying the scene. Ward sat in the centre of a circle of the men and he was telling them a story which they evidently found fascinating.

She envied him his ability to get on so well with

these strange people. It was no wonder he had not been unduly concerned when they came down in the jungle. She had imagined that any Indians they met would be wild, cannibals perhaps. But he must have known differently. She wished he had told her.

When Ward spotted her he beckoned her to join him and the young men moved swiftly to one side, allowing her to pass through.

'What are you doing?' she asked quietly, glancing apprehensively at their audience who all had inane grins on their faces and were gazing at her with intense curiosity.

'I'm explaining how we came to be here,' he said. 'They think I'm very lucky to be travelling with such a beautiful girl.'

Verna looked at him suspiciously, and then again at the men. She recognised some of them as the ones who had joined in their swimming games, and blushed furiously when she realised they had seen her naked.

Not that it made much difference, their womenfolk went around like that all the time. But to Verna it suddenly seemed that they had invaded her privacy, and she was acutely embarrassed.

When one of them came across and handed her a bead necklace, placing it over her head himself, his fingers brushing her breasts as he carefully arranged it, she clutched at Ward involuntarily.

'Tell him to get away,' she said tightly. 'I don't want his presents.'

'You'll hurt his feelings,' he replied, grinning wickedly. 'He doesn't mean anything.'

But Verna was not so sure. She dragged up a smile, however, and then turned to Ward again. 'Can't we go to our hut?' she asked tremulously. 'These men scare me.'

He shook his head, as though finding it difficult to accept her feelings. 'They're a very friendly tribe, Verna, one of the friendliest I've met. You can't rush away now. They're talking about doing a dance for our benefit. You must stay and watch.'

What choice had she? But she made sure that she kept close to Ward. Regardless of what had transpired between them she still needed him, he was her protector, her passport out of this place.

One by one the Indians disappeared, returning shortly afterwards with their faces and bodies painted in alarming red and black patterns. They wore feathered headdresses, feathered armbands and anklets, and carried spears and arrows, and altogether looked a most ferocious lot.

Verna was frankly scared and clutched at Ward, not sure that she agreed with his implicit trust in these warlike people.

But when the dancing began she forgot her fear, gazing with frank interest as they stamped and chanted and sang, growing wilder as the minutes passed, sometimes stopping to give a loud roar and then beginning all over again, arrows and spears held high above their heads, bare feet pounding the earth.

Verna was fascinated and found herself clapping her hands in time to their chanting. Sweat poured down their gleaming bodies as they whirled faster and faster, feet thudding, voices loud and shrill with several ear-piercing shrieks filling the air.

Her feet began to tap and when one of the men held out his hand she let him pull her up and she joined in their dancing, slowly at first, but as she learned their steps her feet moved quicker and quicker until at length she felt as though she was flying through the air.

Eventually, completely exhausted, she collapsed

into a laughing, perspiring heap. Her clothes were saturated yet again, but she felt surprisingly happy and when Ward pulled her up she lifted her face for his kiss—much to the delight of the watching Indians.

They stood round them in a circle and began clapping and chanting, and Ward said, 'They want us to dance—think you can manage it?'

'I doubt it,' she said faintly, 'I'm exhausted.'

He clasped his hands behind her back, holding her against the muscular strength of him. 'I'll hold you up,' he said. 'We mustn't let them down,' and they began their dance.

They skipped and whirled to the encouraging chants of the men, who had now been joined by the women, wondering what all the noise was about. Ward seemed to have an inexhaustible supply of energy, but Verna knew that had it not been for his strong arms she would have succumbed long ago.

At length they gave in, dropping to the floor and shaking their heads when they were asked to continue. 'I'm ready for bed,' she said faintly.

His eyes twinkled and to the obvious approval of the Indian tribe he stood up, lifting Verna effortlessly into his arms and carrying her to their hut.

Verna was aware of the strong beating of his heart, and as she linked her hands round his neck she felt an overwhelming urge to smother his face with kisses.

What would he think? she wondered. But once in the hut he immediately dropped her, and she was glad she had not bothered. His treatment had been nothing more than a front for the Indians.

Disappointing, perhaps, but no more than she should have expected. In any case she had brought it all on herself. She began to climb into her hammock, but Ward said sharply, 'You'd better strip off those wet clothes. You're asking for trouble sleeping in them.'

'And what am I supposed to wear?' she asked huffily. 'These jeans are the only clothes that cover my legs completely. I don't want to wake up a mass of mosquito bites. I'm bad enough already, thank you very much!'

'The Indians have kindly provided us with blankets,' he said quietly, and when she still made no effort to shed her sweat-laden garments, 'Shall I do it for you?'

'No, thanks,' she said tightly. 'Just turn your back.'

He laughed harshly. 'And what the hell have you got to hide that I haven't already seen?'

'It's different here,' she cried wildly. 'This is our bedroom—you don't understand.'

'Oh, I do,' he said, and in the semi-darkness she could tell he was smiling. 'And you've hit on the operative word—*our* bedroom. So far as the Indians are concerned we could be man and wife. In fact we have quite an audience already, if you care to look. Surely you don't want to disappoint them?'

Verna turned and saw the dark shapes of several bodies outside their hut, peering through the slits in the pole structure of the walls. 'Tell them to go away!' she shrieked. 'Haven't they any sense of decency? Don't they respect a person's privacy?'

'You're in the jungle now,' he laughed. 'There's no such thing. Get undressed, and don't be a prude.'

Verna snatched the blanket from him with shaking hands and somehow managed to strip off her clothes while holding it around her. Cocooned in its warmth, she scrambled awkwardly into her hammock.

Ward's hoot of laughter filled the hut. 'What a game! You really do amaze me.'

She glared in the darkness. 'Just because you have no self-respect it doesn't mean we all have to be the same!'

She could see his shadowy shape, completely naked, before he too wrapped himself in his blanket and curled up in the hammock next to her own.

The figures outside melted away and soon there was nothing to be heard but Ward's even breathing and the usual night sounds of droning insects and screeching birds, to which she had gradually become accustomed. They no longer alarmed her and very soon she was asleep too.

When she awoke she felt cold and wet, and for a moment she could not imagine what was wrong. Then she realised it was raining and that the plaited palm fronds above gave little or no protection.

Looking across at Ward, she could see his outline still curled in the blanket, and marvelled that he could sleep when heavy rain was pouring on him.

A flash of lightning illuminated the sky, sending vivid jags of light into their hut, and she cried out in alarm, and woke Ward. He sat up abruptly, immediately taking stock of their situation.

Wind whistled through their leafy roof and Verna shivered uncontrollably, her teeth chattering so that Ward swore violently and rolled out of his bunk.

'There's not much we can do until this rain stops,' he said. 'No point in getting changed, we'll only be soaked again in a few seconds.' He searched in his bag and brought out a bottle of *cachaça*.

'I was saving this for emergencies,' he said grimly. 'Take a swig.'

The burning liquid ran down Verna's throat into her stomach, causing her to cough and choke but at the same time warming her. She handed it back silently. Ward took a mouthful himself, then they sat huddled together on one hammock, waiting for the rain to stop.

As usual it happened as suddenly as it had started, and sunrise followed swiftly. The burning sun took over and their wet clothes and blankets were soon steaming beneath its intense heat. In a matter of minutes they were dry.

Verna took another swim in the lagoon, delighted to find she had it to herself, and over breakfast of eggs, from the few pitiful-looking hens that scratched at the bare earth, she asked Ward whether he intended moving on that day.

'I'd like to,' he said, but, unusually solicitous, added. 'It all depends whether you feel up to it.'

Her eyes narrowed suspiciously. 'I can't believe that you care how I feel.'

He shrugged. 'Believe what you like. The decision is yours.'

'And if I choose to stay then you'll blame me afterwards if something goes wrong?' she ventured sharply.

'Not unless it's your fault,' he said calmly.

She could not help feeling that there was something behind all this. 'We'll move on,' she said decisively. 'The sooner we reach civilisation the sooner I'll be rid of you.'

His lips compressed tightly. 'I'm sorry you feel that way.'

'Are you?' she flared. 'Are you sure you're not taking a perverse delight in dragging me through all this? That you're not hoping that the going won't get tougher so that you can see me suffer even more?'

'Strange as it may seem,' he said quietly, warningly, 'I don't like to see you suffer at all.'

She looked suspiciously into the intense blue of his eyes, but they looked sincere enough, and she wondered whether she could be mistaken, whether he really did care about her. It would all be for the sake of Guy Pemberton, of course, not because of any real feelings so far as she personally was concerned.

'I must be mad,' she said suddenly, 'but I believe you.'

His smile did not quite reach his eyes. 'Thank goodness for that. Go and pack while I have one last word with our mutual friends.'

An hour later they were on their way, Verna again feeling an unutterable disappointment at leaving behind this hospitable race. They had been showered with more gifts; headdresses, bows and arrows, further necklaces, until they became totally embarrassed by the generosity of this tribe.

Verna gave away her handbag mirror and some lipstick and a delicate lace handkerchief, and wished she had something more to offer. But nevertheless the women were grateful and there was sadness all round when they finally left.

The jungle seemed denser and more difficult to penetrate than before and after an hour or so Verna wished she had not been so willing to move on.

Her blisters, which had begun to heal, were rubbed red raw again and each step became painful. Ward, in front as usual, knew nothing of this and hacked through the undergrowth with amazing skill and strength. Verna wondered from where he drew his source of energy. He really was a remarkable man.

Somehow, despite her sore feet, she managed to keep up, and when he eventually suggested they stop for lunch, she said with remarkable calm, 'It's up to you, Ward.'

His glance was suspicious, but when he saw the lines of fatigue on her face he said gently, 'Sit down, Verna. Stop playing the martyr.'

Her legs crumpled beneath her even as he spoke, and she leaned back against the bole of a tree, easing off her shoes, closing her eyes and falling immediately asleep.

The next thing she knew Ward was offering her a steaming cup of black coffee, and rice was cooking on the Primus. She accepted it gratefully and the liquid soothed and relaxed her.

She ate the dried meat and rice ravenously and drank more coffee, and then Ward said they ought to be moving again. But when she tried to put on her shoes her feet were so sore that she winced unintentionally.

She had not wanted to complain, she had intended hiding her discomfort from Ward, but he had already observed her reaction and she knew she could not hide her bleeding feet any longer.

Gently he peeled off her socks, exclaiming aloud when he saw the open wounds. 'In hell's name, why didn't you tell me?' he rasped savagely. 'These could go poisonous, don't you know that? Why do you think I told you not to scratch your mosquito bites? Any open wound is an invitation for infection.'

He cleansed her feet with antiseptic lotion, bandaging them carefully, and then pulling on another pair of his thick socks. With a sharp knife he slit the backs of her shoes so that they would not dig into her heels yet again, and with a spare pair of laces tied them around her instep so they would not fall off.

'Try that,' he said tersely, pulling her upright, watching closely as she experimentally took a few hesitant steps.

'Much better,' she smiled.

'Are you sure?'

She nodded. In point of fact they still hurt, but not so much as they had, and she knew he would not be happy if she held him up any longer.

A little farther they found a narrow track and with the going much easier they made better progress. Constantly, though, Ward stopped to satisfy himself that Verna was in no great pain, and she found his concern touching.

Their path took them alongside a narrow stream for part of the way, which Ward told her was a tributary of the Xingu river. Bright blue water lilies floated among sage-green leaves, the banks were overhung with thick undergrowth and colourful exotic birds appeared from the dark forest.

'Can't we stay here?' asked Verna, feeling tempted by the thought of the cooling water. She was soaked yet again with perspiration and did not know how she managed to force herself on. Only the thought of Ward's sharp tongue kept her legs moving.

He looked far from pleased. 'If you really must. I had hoped to make another few miles.'

'Then you go!' she cried wildly. 'I've had enough for today!'

'You think I'd leave you?' he questioned tersely.

She shot him an angry glance. 'I wouldn't be surprised. You're so damned concerned with getting out of this place you don't care two hoots how I feel. It's me you're supposed to be caring about, in case you'd forgotten. Is it a corpse you're hoping to end up with?'

His fists clenched at his sides and a pulse jerked in his jaw. 'If you carry on like that, I shall do the job myself. For God's sake, Verna, pull yourself together.'

'I've had it,' she said, quietly now. 'I can't go another step.' She swayed and the jungle began to spin before her eyes, and the next second she was in Ward's arms. He sat her down and forced her head between her knees, and after a while she felt better.

He fished out his bottle of *cachaça* and made her take a few gasping swallows, then he looked at his watch. 'Another hour and it'll be dark. Perhaps as well to make camp here after all.'

Yet even so he sounded reluctant. 'I'm much better now,' protested Verna. 'If you want to go on, I think I can manage it.' No way was she going to let him put the blame on her.

But as she made to rise he put a heavy hand on her shoulder. 'Stow it, Verna! You're being stupid. I'd have to be blind or crazy not to see that you're in no condition to take another step today.'

And she did not argue. She was incredibly tired and weak and actually doubted whether she would ever be able to walk again. The heat was unbearable, so thick and dense that it almost choked her. More often than not her breath came in rasping gasps and she had developed a pain in her chest due to constant futile endeavours to drink in some fresh air.

Ward lit a fire and boiled water and she drank strong sweet coffee and revelled in the luxury of doing absolutely nothing. The moving river looked inviting, and she wondered whether it was safe to bathe, supposing of course she could summon up the energy to get there.

They sat in silence watching grey and white herons with their long legs standing in the matted undergrowth. Silver fish jumped out of the water and a flock of parrots streaked past in a blur of colour.

It could be a magical place, if it wasn't for the energy-sapping heat. Verna's lethargy dragged on and on, and the longer she sat the less inclined she felt to move.

She watched dully as Ward prepared a meal, and while it was cooking slung their hammocks and fastened the mosquito netting. What a stalwart character he was at a time like this! With any lesser man she doubted they would have made it.

Unexpectedly her thoughts turned to David, and she could not help smiling as she imagined him in this situation. The heat would have taken its toll out of him as much as her. They would probably not have got out of the jungle alive.

He was a super character, and she was very fond of him, but he in no way matched Ward for toughness and stamina. Even his physique was totally different. David was tall, admittedly, but not powerful. A life of painting and no exercise had slackened his muscles and she knew that in later years he would develop a paunch, and maybe even a double chin, because he put food only second to painting.

'What are you thinking?' asked Ward suddenly. 'It's the first time you've smiled since we left the Indian camp.'

Always totally honest, Verna said, 'I was comparing you with David.'

His eyes narrowed suddenly. 'And?'

'I don't think he'd have survived in this situation.'

'I don't suppose he would,' agreed Ward

amiably. 'Not many men would, unless they've been trained for it.'

'I've survived,' she said heatedly, suddenly wishing she had not told him. 'And I'm a mere woman.'

'But a very remarkable one.' His eyes were enigmatic as they rested upon her face. 'You're tougher than you look, Verna.'

'But not tough enough to keep up with you,' she said bitterly.

His brows rose. 'I never expected you to. You're doing extremely well. I never thought we'd make half the progress we have.'

'Now he tells me!' she mocked. 'And I was dead scared to admit I was tired. I thought you'd blow your top.'

'I probably would have done,' he admitted, smiling wryly. 'But you must agree my method worked. I reckon by nightfall tomorrow at this rate we'll reach the post. And then soon we'll be winging our way home.'

He sounded so confident that Verna believed him. 'You really think so?' I hadn't realised we were so near. No wonder you wanted to press on!'

'It doesn't matter.' He shook his head reassuringly. 'I can tell by the state you're in that you'd never have made it, and I don't think that even I would have the stamina to carry you the last few miles.'

They lapsed into a companionable silence, Ward smoking, Verna watching the lazily moving waters. Afterwards they ate and then Ward suggested an early night. But Verna had not yet tried the tempting waters.

She collected a towel and walked down to the edge of the river, slipping off her shoes and socks and wading in up to her knees. But quickly she was dancing out again, crying for Ward, desperately trying to knock off tiny fishes which clung like leeches to her legs.

'Why didn't you warn me?' she yelled.

'There are some things it's best to find out for yourself,' he said, humour lurking in his eyes. 'Don't panic, you're not hurt.'

After that Verna made do with splashing water carefully over her. It was cooling, but certainly not so refreshing as a dip would have been.

Verna was already in her hammock when the sun set, and the magical vision enchanted her. The sinking orb turned the river to molten gold and the dramatic effects in the sky would have delighted David's artistic eye. Not for the first time she wished she had her camera with her. But it had been left on the plane as unnecessary baggage—another of Ward's stipulations.

Soon afterwards she slept, waking to a pitch black jungle that was so silent it was uncanny. But something had disturbed her. Why else would she have woken in the middle of the night, when she was so tired she had felt as though she could sleep a week?

Her eyes pierced the darkness and she felt an unreasoning cold prickle of fear down her spine. She reached for the gun which Ward always insisted she take to bed with her.

The hard metal felt reassuring beneath her fingers, though she was not sure she would have the courage to use it should it become necessary.

'Ward!' she called in a hoarse whisper.

Her only answer was a snore.

*'Ward!'* she hissed, more loudly this time.

But still he slept on.

She was afraid to shout any louder in case whatever it was that had awaked her should materialise and silence her for ever!

Suddenly the moon sailed from behind a cloud, filtering through the trees, casting vague shadowy shapes over their camp. Verna's eyes scanned the area. Nothing. Absolutely nothing.

A branch moved on the dying fire, sending up a shower of sparks and a flickering flame.

And then she saw it!

Stretched out on a branch immediately above Ward's head was a jaguar. The magnificent beast was as still as the night, only the slits of his golden eyes watchful, turned now on Verna as she moved uneasily in her hammock, clutching her gun, her mouth dry and a cold sweat filming her limbs.

Suddenly came the terrifying bloodcurdling cry of a troop of howler monkeys. They had sensed the danger! Coming on top of her fear of the jaguar, Verna shot bolt upright in her hammock, calling out to Ward.

As she moved the jaguar too became alert, its body tense, its eyes resting on her. She was convinced her end was near and in sheer unadulterated panic she took the gun in both hands, pointed it at the watching animal, closed her eyes, and squeezed the trigger.

# CHAPTER EIGHT

VERNA still had her gun pointed when Ward's voice penetrated her stunned mind.

'Verna, what the hell? *Verna!*'

Slowly she opened her eyes and looked at him, but her body was rigid from fear and she was unable to move a muscle.

He sprang from his bunk and came over, whisking aside the mosquito net and removing the gun carefully from her nerveless fingers.

With a shuddering sigh she collapsed against him. She was alive. She was still alive! 'Oh, Ward,' she cried, 'did I kill it?'

'Kill what, for heaven's sake?' he demanded angrily. 'Have you been dreaming?'

She shook her head wildly. 'It was no dream. I saw this jaguar—right above your hammock. Oh, Ward, I was so frightened!'

'You shot at it? You stupid idiot, why didn't you wake me? Did you wound it? I hope not—nothing can be more dangerous than a wild animal crazed with pain.'

'I don't know,' she said, 'I shut my eyes.'

*'Hell!'* He banged his fist against the trunk of the tree. 'Hell, Verna! Can't you do anything right?'

She needed sympathy, understanding, not anger. Her eyes flashed. 'Would you have preferred I got myself killed—or let him get you—you were right under him?' Her voice was shrill and angry—and still frightened—and she needed Ward to hold her, not shout.

Tears came, but she dashed them away savagely. 'Some protection you were, snoring your head off!'

'I do not snore,' he said tightly, ridiculously. And you could have got us both killed. I'll keep the gun in future. I need no more of your histrionics.'

'I like that!' she cried. 'I reckon I was doing us both a favour. I did call you, in case you're not aware of it. What else was I supposed to do?'

'Let well alone,' he said. 'Unless he was absolutely starving he wouldn't have attacked us.'

'And how was I supposed to know that?' she demanded. 'I'm afraid my education didn't include the ways of the jungle.'

Reaction set in and she began to shiver, her limbs moving uncontrollably, her teeth chattering, no matter how much she tried to stop them.

'Damn!' snarled Ward. He threw a few more twigs on the fire and she climbed down from her hammock, crouching before its encompassing warmth.

He boiled water and made coffee, which she gulped gratefully before handing the cup silently back to him. When at length she felt calmer she said, 'I'm sorry if I did wrong. I acted instinctively.'

'It's all right,' came his grudging response. 'I shouldn't have shouted—but you don't realise how close you came to getting yourself killed. Thank goodness you missed!'

'How do you know I did?'

'We'd have heard him roaring and crashing through the undergrowth. I reckon all you did was scare him away. Go back to bed now. I'll sit up and keep guard—just in case.'

'You mean you're not sure?' Verna's skin began

to crawl again and she edged towards him without even realising it.

He rested his arm across her shoulders. 'Ninety-nine per cent. But I know you won't sleep thinking about it.' He smiled reassuringly. 'Go on, make yourself comfortable. There are still a few hours of darkness left, and I want you fit to travel tomorrow.'

And that was all he cared about, she thought dismally. It was comforting with his arm round her. 'Can't I stay here?' she asked quietly, her eyes wide and guileless. 'I need you. I feel safe in your arms.'

'And I need you,' he cried angrily, 'but I don't think we're talking about the same thing. Stay if you like, but I'm warning you, I won't be responsible for my actions.'

And Verna knew only too well what he meant. 'Perhaps I'd better get into my hammock,' she said sadly, even though her heart beat wildly and she knew that she would have liked nothing better than to spend the rest of the night in his arms. But it would be a wrong move. It could lead to all sorts of consequences.

She missed the tightening of his lips as she broke free and clambered ungainly into the hammock, and it was a long, long time before she went back to sleep.

She lay in the semi-darkness staring at Ward's back as he sat hunched over the fire. Occasionally he would stir to throw on another log, but generally he sat without moving and she wondered what thoughts were going through his mind.

He made no secret of the fact that he desired her, yet she knew the insanity of giving in to him in this wild place. It would be something she would regret all her life. And yet even as she thought this her heart went out to him and her throbbing pulses told their own story.

'Oh, Ward,' she cried silently, 'why does it have to be like this?'

Verna had not thought she would sleep, but somehow she managed to drop off again, waking as the early morning sun began to force back the grey skies.

It was a magical world, holding none of the horrors of the night. Whirls of white mist rose from the river, gossamer webs hung from the trees and grasses, glistening with a thousand drops of shimmering mist. Everything was bathed in a rosy golden glow, and Verna marvelled that anything so beautiful could hide untold danger.

Ward had breakfast cooking and returned a brisk, 'Good morning,' in reply to her own cheerful greeting as she went down to the river for a sketchy wash. He did not sound in a particularly good humour and she wondered whether it was because of his enforced sleepless night, or whether he was still cross with her for using the gun.

'I'm glad you woke early,' he said, when she returned. 'We'll move off as soon as we've eaten.'

'Why the desperate rush?' she asked sharply, a frown of displeasure creasing her forehead.

'Because I want to get this hell of a journey over with,' he returned. 'And so do you, I imagine.'

'Are you trying to say that you've had enough of my company?' Her eyes were overbright and her tone distinctly shrill.

'I think you've had enough of mine.' His face was grim as he spooned rice and beans on to her plate. 'I guess we'll both be glad when the time comes for us to part.'

A lump rose in Verna's throat. It became perfectly clear in that moment that Ward's need of her had been pure and simple lust. If she had not been sure before she was now. He had finally accepted that she would not be a party to his desires and therefore she held no further interest for him.

'Extremely glad,' she said loudly and positively, and picking up her plate began to eat as fast as she could, pushing down the food, swallowing desperately even though it almost choked her.

She jumped up immediately she had finished and took their plates to the river. Ward had the hammocks packed and everything ready when she returned.

He set off at a crippling pace, so that Verna was limp and exhausted before they had even travelled a half hour. Her steps grew slower and slower and she lagged further and further behind. The heat grew more intense by the second and she even found it difficult to appreciate the beauty of their surroundings.

Golden shafts of sunlight illuminated their path, colourful butterflies flitted about her head, flocks of parrots darted through the thick jungle in occasional brilliant flashes. Enormous spider's webs festooned their path, shining with droplets of water, sticky to her face as she brushed past them. Leaf ants, carrying leaves four times their size, crossed the track in front of her.

But Ward blundered on and she was compelled to follow, staggering like a drunken man. Perspiration ran into her eyes and mouth and her clothes were sodden against her skin.

In the end she gave up, sitting on a dead tree trunk and burying her head in her hands. Let him go on, she thought. It was doubtful that he would even miss her. Tears of self-pity mingled with sweat and she had never felt so alone in her life.

Didn't it occur to him that she was a mere female? That she was unable to keep up with his inexhaustible supply of energy? Had the man no feelings at all?

It was several minutes before she heard him tramping back through the undergrowth. Even then she did not look up, though she was aware that he stood over her, and could imagine the fury on his face.

'We'll get nowhere at this rate!' he thundered, making her jump with the suddenness of his words.

'I can't keep up,' she said flatly.

'You've done it before, why not today?' he rapped.

'You haven't surged on like a man demented,' she cried, looking at him finally, and shrinking when she saw the hardness in his eyes. 'What is it, a marathon last day? Are you trying to prove something, or simply trying to bring our association to an end as quickly as you can? I know you're eager, but I didn't realise exactly to what extent.'

'Now you do,' he rasped, and taking her hand yanked her to her feet. 'You've had your rest, let's go.'

She wrenched free, eyes blazing furiously. 'I'll go when I'm good and ready, thank you! If you want to leave me here then that's all right by me. I think I've learned enough about survival to make my own way from now on.'

'You think so?' His brows rose mockingly.

'Yes, I do,' she said tightly, chin thrust, mouth set determinedly.

He shrugged. 'Very well, my brave lady. The choice is yours. I'll leave you the haversack, you'll need it.' He slipped it from his shoulders and held it out.

Verna took it hesitantly. She had not really expected him to agree, but was sure she would not back down now. He would gloat, and she would not like that, not one little bit.

Without another word he strode away, turning only once to look at her with questing eyes.

'I've not changed my mind,' she called bravely.

His lips curled in wry humour, then he shrugged and turned and was soon lost to sight, though she could hear his feet as he tramped through the tangled growth.

Verna tried to tell herself that she was not afraid, that she had come this far with no mishap, it would be easy to carry on. Ward had said they had only one more day's walking—and presumably this track was the one she had to follow. He would have told her if it wasn't, surely?

She slung the bag across her shoulders. It was heavier than she had realised. How on earth had Ward managed with this pack on his back for so many days?

She made slow progress and by noon, when the heat was at its most intense, she had travelled no more than a couple of miles. She flung herself down, uncaring for once whether there were ants or spiders, and went to sleep.

When she awoke she instinctively looked for Ward, until she remembered he had gone. He had deserted her! She was in this grim jungle, alone, defenceless, and more than likely she would never get out of it alive.

Why, oh, why had she been so stubborn? Why had she warred with him when the most rational thing to do in a place like this was to be friends?

She sucked a lime and picked at a piece of dried meat, unable to face the thought of struggling to light a fire and cook herself something nourishing.

Another half hour's walking and the track petered out. Verna stood uncertainly. Now which way? And how on earth was she going to hack her way through the jungle?

A search of the haversack revealed no knife. Ward must have taken it with him. Think rationally, she told herself, as panic welled. If Ward has the knife he must have cut a rough path.

It was several minutes before she discovered his trail. By this time tears ran freely down her face and she deeply regretted ever saying she could manage alone.

Sheer bravado, that was all it had been. Surely Ward must have known that? Why had he accepted so eagerly? Why had he not told her she was being stupid and that no way could she cope with the rigours of jungle travel?

He was callous and uncaring and she doubted he would even have a twinge of conscience if she died out here. He would say good riddance.

Anger lent her strength, pure furious anger, and she tramped on, bitterly cursing Ward with every step. When a snake slithered across the path in front of her she froze in horror, but bit back a scream which would have told him that she was not really brave.

Yard by yard she pushed herself on, following Ward's tracks, but feeling more desperately lonely with each passing minute. He might not have been much company, but at least he was someone, and he knew how to cope in an emergency!

As the sun began to sink Verna realised that there was no way she would make the post that day. Thoughts of an entire night spent alone made her tingle with terror, but somehow it had to be got through, and there was no point in being faint-hearted.

She found a suitable spot and gathered twigs and dried leaves, then realised she had nothing with which to light the fire. Ward always used his lighter—and he kept that in his pocket. Did rubbing two sticks together really work? she wondered, before deciding it was not even worth trying.

Instead she made do with some more of the now unappetising dried meat and the last of the guavas, swallowing her anti-malaria pill last of all.

Had Ward a supply with him? she asked herself, and marvelled that she could be so concerned. Serve him right if he did catch malaria, she thought nastily. It would be what he deserved for deserting her in a place like this!

It was pitch black before she remembered that she had not fixed her hammock, and she struggled in vain for a good half hour before giving it up as a bad job. It had all looked so easy when Ward did it.

Tears of frustration and rage ran down her face as she curled beneath a tree and kept her fingers metaphorically crossed that she would not be eaten alive by the army of insects who came into their own at night.

Far away, howler monkeys set up their chilling cries, parrots screamed shrilly and thousands of tree frogs croaked in unison. Verna was terrified and lay tense and uncomfortable on her leafy bed, knowing instinctively that she was not going to get any sleep that night.

When she heard a tramping through the undergrowth she went rigid with fear, convinced it was the jaguar she had attempted to shoot. A single red glow hove into sight. She had shot his eye! she thought in panic—and now this one-eyed monster was after her.

She watched transfixed, shaking like a jelly, feeling her blood run cold. When she could stand it no longer she shot to her feet, one wild scream following another, as she headed into the pitch blackness of the jungle.

Footsteps crashed after her and she ran faster, her heart pounding in her ears. When she tripped and fell she covered her head with her hands. This was it, the end of Verna Pemberton.

Suddenly there was silence. Every nerve end tingled and she knew there was something behind her, she could hear the quiet sound of its breathing, feel the tenseness that crackled in the air around them.

And then Ward's voice cut into the stillness. 'I'm glad to see you coping so admirably.'

She twisted round and glared, relief and anger mingling. He drew on his cigar, the faint glow illuminating his face so that she became aware of the sardonic smile.

'You!' she accused hotly. 'Why didn't you speak? Why didn't you say something? I thought you were——'

'A wild animal?' he jeered. 'It looks to me as though you're not quite so courageous as you made out. Are you still sure you want to travel alone?'

'Oh, go to hell!' she snapped viciously.

'You mean join you?' His voice was full of humour. 'It is a hell of a place, I agree, especially when you're not fully equipped, and you're alone, and you don't know what you will find round the next corner.'

She struggled to her feet, her fear in no way lessened by his appearance. His baiting comments needled her and she wished he had kept away.

'You're not much of a gentleman for leaving me,' she cried, 'knowing the dangers that are involved.'

He shrugged easily. 'It was your idea. I never force myself where I'm not wanted.'

'And you're not wanted now,' she returned,

brushing past him and marching back to her camp.

'You mean you'd rather I go and leave you to spend the night on your own?'

'Yes,' she cried wildly, and then less aggressively, 'unless you want to stay? I don't want to be unsociable.'

'A good excuse,' he smiled, bending down and putting a light to the fire she had built.

It soon blazed brightly and she was able to see clearly the mocking good humour on his face. It irritated her beyond measure. He was openly laughing at her inadequacy.

But she needed him, even though she was reluctant to admit it. Without Ward she would be unable to exist in this living green hell.

Silently he slung their hammocks, giving Verna the intact mosquito net, taking for himself the one she had ruined with her gun shots.

'Thank you,' she said quietly, climbing in and watching him through the gauzy net of her covering. She was grateful to him for coming back, but found it impossible to express her gratitude.

His confident arrogance irritated her beyond words, and although she readily admitted that he was a man to surpass all men, and that she was dangerously close to falling in love with him, she had no intention of letting him see how she felt. He would take advantage, she was certain. Any man in the same situation would.

She watched as Ward climbed into his hammock and then her eyes closed and she knew no more until the sun was high in the sky, filtering through their leafy roof, and Ward was impatiently waiting for them to set off.

'You should have woken me,' she said apologetically.

'I did try.' His lips were tight. 'You were sleeping the sleep of the dead. Was yesterday such an ordeal?'

She shrugged. 'Not really. As a matter of fact I quite enjoyed it.' Why did she lie? He must know that it was all an act, another pretence of bravado.

'I'm afraid there's nowhere you can wash,' he told her. 'You didn't make a very good choice for a night's camp.'

'It doesn't matter,' she returned tonelessly. She had become accustomed to feeling sweaty and grimy, and although the thought of a bath was enticing, all she wanted at this moment was to get out of this place and to hell with her appearance.

He handed her a cup of coffee and some fruit. 'A couple of hours and we should be at the post. With luck you'll be able to get a good meal then. How are you feeling?'

'Such concern is touching,' she said tightly. 'I feel how I look—tired, dirty, worn out and close to tears. Is that answer enough?'

He grimaced ruefully. 'I'm sorry, Verna. I realise how hard it's been for you.' He put a tentative arm about her shoulders. 'But it won't be for much longer. Think you can stick it out?'

With you beside me, she thought. But she merely nodded and shrugged away from him. She was not too exhausted not to feel any reaction to his touch. It set her pulses racing and filled her with an insane desire to fling herself at him and sob her heart out against his chest.

How would he react? she wondered. Would he think it sheer hysteria, or would he realise how deeply emotionally involved she had become?

Now that the end of their journey was in sight Verna found new reserves of energy, and amazed herself by keeping up with Ward's steady pace.

And as though he regretted leaving her he continually assured himself that she was coping, stopping frequently for rests, checking that she was capable of continuing.

His concern made her realise how deep were her feelings for him, and it became an effort to hide the love shining in her eyes. At least he would mistake her quivering limbs for weakness. He would never guess after the way she had behaved that she was falling more deeply in love with him by the minute.

When Verna saw a cluster of wooden huts in a jungle clearing it was impossible to stop the tears from rolling down her cheeks. She turned to Ward happily. 'Is that it? Is that the post?'

He nodded, smiling too. 'I was waiting for you to spot them. What does it feel like to know that your troubles are almost over?'

'Wonderful!' she cried, grinning from ear to ear, and beginning to run, stopping short only when she saw a group of Indians standing watching. The men wore tattered khaki shorts and the women faded cotton dresses, the children as usual were completely naked.

Ward was welcomed like an old friend and Verna looked at him questioningly. 'I have been here before,' he admitted. 'I once brought a group of missionaries.'

Verna was scrutinised closely, as she had been by each of the other tribes they had met, and then accepted as a friend of Ward's and invited into their huts.

They were palm-thatched and built on stilts, reached by a flight of rough wooden steps, the walls reaching only half way up, the rest open to the elements.

They were allocated a hut for their own use and

one of the Indians brought heavy cloth hammocks and fastened them to the supporting beams.

'I didn't think we were going to stay,' whispered Verna, dismayed at the look of permanency.

'We may have to spend a few nights,' shrugged Ward. 'It depends when the next plane is due. I've asked the wireless operator to send a message explaining our predicament, and if it's at all possible a special plane will be sent out for us. Otherwise we wait for one bringing supplies.'

Verna looked downcast and was almost ready to burst into tears.

'At least there's no more walking,' he said cheerfully. 'You'll be comfortable here. We're close to the river for washing, there are toilets, and a proper eating house. It's all quite civilised.'

'For Indians maybe,' she cried. 'But I thought we were so close to the end of our journey—and now——'

'You've discovered that you're not rid of me yet,' he said grimly. 'Sorry, Verna, but there's not much I can do about it. I've done my best for you. If that's not good enough, then——'

'I'm sorry.' She touched his arm urgently, unable to bear the harshness of his tone. 'I'm ungrateful. It's just that I've had almost as much as I can take.'

'Of me—or the jungle?' he queried brusquely. 'For heaven's sake go and get freshened up and put on some clean clothes, maybe you'll feel better.'

He left the hut, and fighting back the tears Verna searched for a towel and shirt. She would wash her jeans before she bathed. At least there was no problem about them drying, although she doubted they would ever be the same again.

It was impossible to get them clean in the river

water and they smelled distinctly musty from their many soakings. Back in London she would never have entertained the idea of putting such revolting objects next to her skin. Necessity had certainly changed her sense of values!

There were several women doing their washing in the river and Verna joined them, pounding her jeans and shirt before draping them on the surrounding bushes.

She felt better after her swim and the thought of remaining here for a day or two was not quite so abhorrent.

Delicious smells came from the eating house as she made her way back to camp, and she looked inside, discovering to her surprise a narrow room with a long table covered with oilcloth, and benches.

Next to it was a kitchen where an old Indian woman was cooking great chunks of golden meat over a fire built on a high platform. Beside it were clay ovens—and it did indeed look more civilised than anything Verna had yet seen in the jungle.

Ward appeared and introduced her to an American nurse who was doing voluntary medical work at the post. It came as a shock to see another white woman, but soon she and Verna were deep in animated conversation.

Kate, as she was called, told Verna that she had been here for twelve months and loved the work. She was a lot older, with a leathery, deeply tanned face. There was a serenity about her features that had a calming influence on Verna, and as they sat for their meal she felt much happier than she had done in days.

When news was brought to Ward that a plane would be arriving the following day to take them to Belém, she was so happy that she burst into tears.

The Indians looked amazed, but Ward smiled and understood—and she was glad.

After their lunch they strolled around the village watching families set off down to the river to fish in canoes dug out of tree trunks, and women and girls pounding maize and manioc.

A few scraggy dogs turned watchful eyes on them, chewing away at well-cleaned bones, naked children ran at their heels, and all in all it was a happy domesticated scene, and because Verna knew that this was the end of their journey she was quite content.

In their hut that night she felt very close to Ward, and as he sat smoking a last cigar she said, 'I apologise if I've been like a bear with a sore head these last few days.'

'Forget it,' he growled. 'For a woman you didn't do too badly.'

'I thought I did jolly well,' she returned, mildly irritated by his offhand manner.

He looked at her through the thin haze of smoke. 'If I hadn't kept pushing you we'd still be somewhere out there.'

'Maybe,' she admitted. 'There were times when I felt like curling up and dying. But I had faith in you, even if I didn't always show it, and I'll be eternally grateful.'

'Eternity is a long time,' he said slowly. 'You ought to think twice before you make rash statements like that. I might be tempted to make you prove it one of these fine days.'

His blue eyes were fixed on her face, the glimmer from the paraffin lamp, fixed on the central pole, revealing the intensity of his gaze. She felt slightly uneasy.

'In fact,' he continued, 'it might not be a bad idea to show some of your gratitude right now. I could certainly do with a woman in my arms.'

She was tempted, far more than he would ever know, but her eyes flashed angrily. 'Then go and take your pick from out there,' she cried rashly. 'There's enough of them, and I guess you'll find them more willing than you're ever likely to find me.'

'I don't know,' he said casually. 'I have a feeling that your protests are a defence, sheer bravado, just like when you said you were capable of coping in the jungle alone. I have half a mind to put you to the test, just like I did then.'

'What do you mean?' she snapped.

'You don't really think I let you caper off alone? I was watching you, my dear Verna, every inch of the way. I found your attempts pathetic to say the least. You'd never have made it here, you do know that?'

'No, I don't!' she snapped. 'You're making it up. You were ahead of me—I watched you go.'

He shrugged lazily. 'I let you think so. But I must admit you are one brave lady. You have spunk. It's a pity it's not backed up with capability.'

'Oh, I hate you!' she cried, dashing across the room and pummelling her fists against his chest. 'You enjoy making me feel uncomfortable. You get a kick out of my lack of knowledge, my inability to cope in emergencies. It's not my fault I haven't been brought up the hard way.'

He caught her wrists, holding them together with one large hand, then hooking the other behind her neck he pulled her close so that her eyes were mere inches away from his own.

'I'd almost forgotten your mother's "Don't

Trust Men" campaign. I must admit she certainly did a good job on you. I've never met a woman so coldly uninterested in men as you appear to be.'

'And it spikes your ego, does it?' she fumed. 'It won't help trying to take me by force!'

Ward stilled for a moment. 'I would never do that. When a woman comes to me she does so willingly.'

'Then why are you holding me now?' Verna's emotions were in turmoil. She desperately wanted to give in to him. She needed to feel his arms about her, the lean strength of his body against her own.

She ached for his love with a hunger she had never before experienced, her body pulsed with desire and she knew that if she did not get free within the next few seconds it would be all over. He would have won. She would go to him voluntarily, and his crow of triumph would be more than she could stand.

'I'm preventing you hitting me,' he said, his blue eyes daring her to deny the truth behind his words.

'Then you can let me go,' she said quietly. 'I have no more fight left in me.'

Mocking brows rose. 'A pity. You look very beautiful when your eyes are flashing fire. You appeal to me when you're angry. I want to dominate you, to possess you.'

His voice deepened and his eyes became glazed with desire. 'I want to pull you into my arms and make wild and uninhibited love. Verna, I want you.'

Verna trembled beneath his touch. There was no doubting he meant every word, and she throbbed with a longing to give herself to him.

Her lips parted and she gazed up at him wonderingly. With a groan he crushed her to him, his lips taking hers with a consummate passion that left her dizzy and gasping for breath.

She no longer felt the need to fight. This was where she belonged. Her hands reached up and touched his shoulders, felt the powerful muscles tense beneath her fingers. And then her hands crept behind his head, mingling in the springy waves of his hair, pulling him unashamedly closer, arching her body, unwittingly telling him that she too needed him.

His lips trailed fire down the slim column of her throat, and his feverish hands tore away the thin cotton of her shirt, exposing her breasts taut and proud.

With a desperate urgency his mouth possessed the hardened nipples, and a moan of sheer pleasure escaped Verna's lips. Convulsively she moved herself against him, realising that only Ward could assuage this unbearable ache that filled her body.

When gently he pushed her away, she mouthed a protest. 'Ward, no, I want you to love me. I—I need you, as you need me.'

'No,' he said, and her breath caught in her throat at the smouldering darkness of his eyes. 'I would never forgive myself. I've just discovered I do have a conscience after all. You don't know what you're doing, little Verna. You would hate yourself afterwards—and me too—and I couldn't stand that.'

With this surprising statement he left the hut. Abruptly and without looking back, and Verna felt bereft and wondered what she had done wrong.

## CHAPTER NINE

SHAME and embarrassment filled Verna as she realised how she had offered herself to Ward—and he had rejected her! It made her wonder whether this hadn't been his aim all along. Had he intended breaking through her carefully erected barriers and then crushing her by denying her the love that she craved?

It was a new experience and one that she did not like, and she felt that she hated Ward Levitt very much indeed. Even so, it did not ease the pain in her breast, and regardless of her feelings at that moment she still desperately felt an overwhelming urge to be loved by him.

It was ironic, this realisation that at last she had met a man whom she felt she could love, and he had spurned her! Her mother had been right all along—men were no good. She had been a fool to let herself become involved.

Except that she had had no choice. It was something that had happened, a love that had grown without her realising it—until it was too late.

She swore explosively and clambered into her hammock. Damn Ward! Damn all men!

'Never make the fatal mistake of becoming involved,' her mother had said. How right she was, and how Verna wished she had heeded her advice.

She tried to sleep, but this new awareness of Ward kept her mind active and no matter how she attempted to banish him from her thoughts he insidiously crept in, until her head was a turmoil and her whole body ached to be loved by him.

When much later he came back into the hut she pretended to be asleep, watching through half-closed eyes as he climbed into his own hammock.

Minutes later he was asleep, and it piqued her to see that their earlier scene had not disturbed him in the least. A game, that was all it had been to him. The only thing in his favour was that at least he had been honourable, and not taken what she had offered.

Her face flamed in the darkness. How could she have been so blatant? What must he have thought? And how could she face him tomorrow?

But when daylight broke there was little time to consider her feelings. She went down to the river to bathe and then breakfasted on eggs and thin pancakes of coarsely ground maize flour, followed by coffee.

Minutes later their plane arrived, landing on the thin strip of runway cleaved in the virgin forest. Verna had not expected it so early, remembering Brazilian time, but she was relieved all the same.

The pilot, a young, tough-looking Brazilian, tanned to a deep bronze, and wearing jeans and a denim shirt, eyes hidden behind black sunglasses, seemed in a hurry. No sooner had he landed than he ushered Ward and Verna aboard.

It was a much bigger plane than Ward's and she felt a whole lot safer. At last it looked as though they were going to reach Belém—and Guy Pemberton, the father she had never known existed.

Quite naturally her thoughts turned to this man, and she wondered whether he really was her father. There did not seem much doubt, yet she could not quite get over the fact that in all her nineteen years he had never once tried to contact her.

And why had her mother said he was dead?

What had gone wrong between them for her to cut him out of her life completely? It was something that only Guy Pemberton could answer. She fetched from her handbag the photograph that Ward had given to her, studying the man's amazing likeness to herself, and feeling at long last an overwhelming urge to meet him.

Up until now this projected meeting had all seemed so remote, so unreal. She had never quite been able to convince herself that it would happen.

And now suddenly it was a matter of hours away. Her heartbeats quickened and she tucked the photo back, conscious all at once that Ward was watching her.

'Feeling nervous?' he asked, the first words he had spoken directly to her that morning, the first words they had in fact exchanged since last night.

She nodded. 'It's quite something at my age to discover you have a father you know nothing about. What if we don't get on? What if he doesn't like me, or I don't like him?'

Ward smiled reassuringly. 'Don't put obstacles in your path before you've even met him! Guy's a great person, you can't help but like him. And he's set his heart on finding you—there's no chance that he'll be disappointed. I can state that quite categorically. Having lived with you these last few days I know that you're exactly the sort of daughter he was expecting.'

Verna eyed him guardedly. 'I'm not certain I know what you mean.'

He grinned. 'Independent, stubborn, beautiful, and beneath it all a warm, loving woman. What better combination could he ask for?'

Not entirely sure that he was not mocking her, Verna commented, 'You seem to have changed your opinion of me. I thought you said I was a cold fish.'

'A false front,' he said brightly. 'An image projected to defend yourself against the masculine race. But like everyone, you're not infallible. There's a chink in your armour—and I must admit I was glad to discover it. I'd have been disappointed if you really had been the ice-maiden you purported to be.'

'I can't see that it would have made any difference to you,' said Verna sceptically. 'Except to damage your male conceit.'

His lips quirked. 'You think it would worry me if I didn't get through to you?'

She nodded emphatically. 'Why else have you bothered? I certainly didn't give you any encouragement.'

'You intrigued me,' he said, eyes glinting wickedly.

'So I was right, you were trying to prove a theory?' She spoke her thoughts out loud.

'Is that what you think?' He looked disappointed and turned away abruptly, saying something to the pilot, and then looking down at the landscape and ignoring Verna.

So why should it annoy him? she asked herself. What difference did it make? She shrugged mentally and sat back in her seat, trying to relax, but finding it extremely difficult to ignore the virile and dangerously attractive man at her side.

He was so totally male, so vitally disturbing. Even thinking about him made her pulses quicken, and she was quite sure that he knew exactly what effect he had on her.

It was disquieting, to say the least. She had always been so proud of her ability to keep her feelings hidden—and now this man had taken them in one hand and thrown them wide open for all to see.

She was vulnerable, and it hurt, and she wished herself a thousand miles away. Stealing occasional glances at his rugged, tanned face, she wondered whether she would ever quite be able to harden her heart to him.

It would be difficult, him being her father's neighbour. They would be sure to see each other on different occasions. Would she be able to keep up a front of being totally uninterested in him?

She doubted it. And if that proved to be the case the only solution would be to return to England, whether she hurt her father by so doing or not.

The sky was a clear light blue and below them the jungle stretched for interminable miles, a thousand shades of green peopled by strange tribes and exotic birds—a place where she had discovered her love—a place she would remember all her life.

The journey took several hours, during which time they flew over impenetrable jungle, criss-crossed by a maze of rivers, and dodged several terrifying electric storms.

Verna was indescribably glad when the pilot announced they had almost reached Belém. She sat nervously on the edge of her seat, glancing at Ward, giving him a weak, apprehensive smile, relieved when he responded. She had been afraid that their uncomfortable silence would continue right up until the time she met her father.

And she needed Ward. She needed his moral support more than anything. This was a big moment in her life and she was not sure that she was capable of handling it alone.

Ward shook the pilot's hand, thanking him profusely for rescuing them, and Verna was so grateful that she flung her arms round his neck in an unusually demonstrative gesture, kissing him warmly on each cheek.

*'De nada,'* he said, grinning broadly.

'He said, "It's nothing",' explained Ward, 'but I reckon you've made his day.'

He hired a car at the airport and soon they were driving through the city streets, lined with beautiful eighteenth-century colonial Portuguese buildings and churches. They were painted in pastel blues and greens, pinks and yellows, and after the green primitiveness of the jungle it seemed like heaven.

'How far is it to my—my father's house?' Verna enquired tentatively.

'A few minutes.'

'Have you let him know that we're safe?'

'I did ask the radio operator at the post to try and get a message through, but whether it reached Guy I have no idea. We'll soon find out.'

'He'll be terribly shocked if he doesn't know,' said Verna.

'Pleasantly, not terribly,' amended Ward. 'He'll be so delighted. I can't wait to see his face.'

Verna was on edge. Now that their meeting was so close she was afraid. 'He might not like me.'

Ward sighed impatiently. 'There you go again! What the hell's the matter with you? It's unlike you to be apprehensive. When we first met I was impressed by your positive manner, you were always so very much in control of yourself. What do you think Guy is, some monster who eats little girls like you for lunch?' He reached across and took her hand. 'Relax, you'll get on just fine. He might be shocked by your appearance, but nevertheless it will make no difference to his feelings for you.'

Verna gripped his hand hard. 'You won't leave me, Ward?'

He shook his head. 'No, Verna, I'll be there.'

Minutes later he pulled up outside a pair of iron gates. Beyond was a large white single-storied house. Guard dogs patrolled the grounds. 'He lives here?' she asked breathlessly, eyeing the vicious-looking alsatians with some trepidation.

Ward nodded, and blew his horn twice. 'I'm afraid the dogs are a necessity. Robbery, especially armed robbery, is an unfortunate part of life here.'

A houseboy came running and when he saw Ward he grinned from ear to ear and opened the gates, speaking in fast Portuguese.

The dogs knew Ward and after a short enthusiastic greeting obeyed his command to sit, though Verna was not so sure she liked the way they looked at her. As they made their way up to the house she kept close to Ward's side, frequently looking back over her shoulder.

A deep verandah ran the length of it, shaded from the heat of the sun. The windows were shuttered and although it was elegant it also looked remote and unlived-in. Verna was not sure that she liked what she saw.

Once inside, though, it was different. The clean coolness of the air-conditioning was like a balm and everywhere was spotless, with beautiful well-polished furniture and over all an aura of wealth.

Verna became immediately aware of their hippie-like appearance. Her jeans were almost falling apart and although she had bathed that morning the heat in the plane had been so intense she knew she must be sweat-grimed, her hair lank and unattractive.

An inner door opened and she watched hypnotically as Guy Pemberton came towards them. He was exactly as in the photograph.

He looked at Ward and Verna, then went pale

and stumbled. Ward shot forward and took his arm.

'I thought you were dead,' said the white-haired man faintly.

'You can't kill me off as easily as that,' said Ward strongly. 'You should know that, Guy. We had a bit of engine trouble, that's all, and we've been stuck in the interior. I tried to get a message to you yesterday, but I presume it didn't arrive.'

But Guy was hardly listening. He was looking at Verna with wonder in his green eyes, as if he could not believe that here at last was the daughter he had been denied all these years.

And watching him, Verna knew without a shadow of doubt that this man was her father. Some intangible thread drew them together, and she walked into his arms as if in a trance.

'My child!' Tears filled the old man's eyes. 'My own Verna, after all these years. I can hardly believe it!'

And then they were crying together, clinging as if their very life depended on it, and when Verna looked round Ward had gone.

But there was suddenly no need of him. She and Guy had lots and lots of talking to do, a whole lifetime to catch up on. He was all she needed right at this moment. He was her father, her family, and she loved him very much.

She found it amazing that she could love a man she had only just met, and she knew there was a great deal she had to learn about him, but for the moment it was sufficient that they had found each other.

'Verna, my own dear child!' He held her as though he never wanted to let her go. 'There's so much I want to know, I want to start talking right at this very moment. But you must be tired, and you need a bath and clean clothes.'

Verna pulled a wry face. 'I have no clothes—Ward made me leave them in the plane. He said we must travel light.'

'Don't worry about that,' he said. 'You shall have all the clothes you want—more than you want. Verna, I'm going to spoil you shamelessly for the rest of my life.'

He was dangerously close to tears again and Verna hugged him. 'Father, oh, Father! Why didn't my mother tell me about you?'

His eyes filled with pain. 'Never mind that now, child. Go and have your bath. We'll talk later.'

A dark-skinned maid appeared and led Verna along a corridor where a marble bath was already filling with warm water. It was deep and scented and the best bath Verna could ever remember having in her life.

She lay for what seemed hours, letting the sweat and grime of the last few days soak away, lathering her hair, feeling a sensual enjoyment in the silky water against her skin.

With a giant-sized fluffy green towel she dried herself and smoothed on body lotion. Scrutinising her reflection in the mirror, she marvelled that she looked so well considering all she had gone through.

Her hair was several shades lighter, its curls bouncing back to life, her skin was a deep honey, her eyes bright and clear, and her tiredness had surprisingly disappeared.

In an adjoining room she found a cotton dress laid out. It was not exactly the height of fashion, and she guessed that it belonged to the maid who had run her bath, but at least it was clean and delicately perfumed, and she could not have felt any better had she been wearing a gown that had cost a fortune.

Guy was waiting, hovering in the corridor outside, and he took her arm immediately she appeared and led her into a comfortable sitting room.

'Are you hungry?' he asked, 'or thirsty? Do you want to go to bed, or can we talk first? Verna, you can't imagine how often I've dreamt of this moment, how many times I've told myself that it was all a foolish notion, that trying to trace you was a sheer impossibility.'

She smiled, curling up beside him on the deep settee. 'Ward told me that you'd employed private investigators. It's a pity you didn't think of asking Ward in the first place. It would have saved you all that money.'

'Money means nothing to me,' he said carelessly. 'I would willingly give everything I possess just to have you at my side. I offered a reward, do you know that? And you'd be surprised at the number of girls who turned up claiming to be my daughter.'

'Then how do you know that I'm genuine?' she teased, touching his face gently, half inclined to believe that this *was* all a dream, that soon she would wake up in her London flat and Jenny would be there and nothing would be changed.

'Instinct,' he smiled gently. 'I knew the moment I saw you that you were my daughter—and you felt it too, I could tell. An indefinable something drew us together, and no one—no one, Verna—is going to part us again.'

'Mother told me you were dead,' she said sadly. 'Why did she do that?'

He hung his head. 'I brought it on myself, I'm afraid. I loved your mother very dearly, but I also loved my work. I'd never married, you see. I was fifty when I met Pamela, I guess I'd become rather selfish.

'I owned a thriving import and export business which took up a lot of my time. Pamela was jealous of the hours I spent at work, and unfortunately I didn't realise it, not until it was too late.

'She accused me of loving my work more than I did her. This was untrue, of course, but I'm afraid I didn't realise how deeply she felt, not until I discovered she was entertaining other men in my house.'

Verna was shocked. 'My mother did that? I can't believe it! She never had any men friends, not to my knowledge. She seemed to hate them, said they were never to be trusted.'

He shook his head unhappily. 'She found out the hard way that they were only interested in her because they thought she was rich. They used her, Verna, and then when they found there was nothing in it for them they left.'

'She told me never to get involved,' admitted Verna. 'I guessed something had happened, but she never told me what. I thought it might have had something to do with you. But I never knew you were still alive. How could she have been so cruel as to deprive me of my own father?'

'Pamela was a law unto herself,' he explained. 'She swore when she left me that she would never let me see you again. At first I tried and I could, of course, have got the courts to force her to allow me access. In fact, I was supposed to see you, but because I still loved her I didn't want to hurt her. So I cleared out of the country, started another business here. It was the hardest decision of my life and I've spent many unhappy hours wondering whether I did the right thing.

'I still can't believe that you're here, that you're mine, that I still have a part of Pamela to remember her by. You're like your mother in some respects.'

Verna felt deeply sorry for this man who had given up so much, and who still loved the woman he had married despite all she had done. 'Father,' she said passionately, 'if it's within my power I'll make up to you all the unhappiness she's caused.'

'You've already done that, my child,' he said, his eyes glowing with contentment. 'Your coming with Ward, your agreeing to see me even though you had no proof that I was your father—that means a lot. I had no idea Pamela had denied my existence. It was a very cruel thing for her to do. I didn't realise she hated me quite so much.'

'Please don't think about it,' said Verna. 'Mother gave me a good life, at least you can be thankful to her for that. I have no complaints. I was very distressed when she died.'

'A motor accident, I believe the solicitor said?' He looked suddenly very old. 'I wish I'd seen her just once more.'

'I'd like a drink,' said Verna suddenly. It was all becoming too much for her father—he looked ill, and she was afraid for his health.

He smiled ruefully. 'How forgetful of me! But of course.' He rang a bell and a maid appeared, a different one this time. He spoke to her in fluent Portuguese and she ran away willingly, darting Verna an inquisitive glance as she did so.

Coffee arrived shortly afterwards—in the inevitable tiny cups with fine sugar and no milk. Verna had become accustomed to this beverage now and drank thirstily.

Her father sat and watched, a benign expression on his face. 'Tell me,' he said at length, 'what do you think of Ward? Isn't he a fine man?'

'He's a very capable man,' she admitted grudgingly. 'He seemed to know a lot about the jungle. I really thought when his plane developed trouble and we were forced to land that it was the end of the road. If it hadn't been for his inexhaustible supply of energy, and his knowledge, and the fact that he was prepared for such an eventuality, I don't think we would have made it.'

'Ward's a skilled man,' he admitted. 'What he doesn't know about the jungle isn't worth knowing. He takes expeditions up the Amazon and into the rain forests there. He has a charmed life. He's been at death's door many times, but always comes out on top. I'm very fond of him, he's been like a son to me all these years.'

It was a revelation to discover that Ward was something of an explorer, as well as running his business empire. Though Verna was not entirely surprised. His calm acceptance, his knowledge of the jungle, all should have told her. Why had he not told her himself that he was an expert? she wondered. She would have felt so much safer!

Dinner was a dream that night. The cook, Carolina, a big motherly type, created a mouth-watering dish of spicy crab, and an incredible boiled duck which they washed down with a light Brazilian wine.

Afterwards, Verna was more than ready for bed and it was bliss to lie between clean cotton sheets and feel the luxury of a sprung mattress, and know that no mosquitoes or bugs were waiting to bite her.

She stretched luxuriously like a cat and fell asleep within seconds. When she awoke and looked at the tiny gilt clock on her bedside table she was shocked to discover that she had slept for over fourteen hours.

The shuttered room was cool and dark and she lay there for a few minutes longer, recalling her meeting with her father, and marvelling that they had got on so well. He really was a wonderful person, and she could not help feeling a bitterness towards her mother for keeping secret the fact that he was alive and well and living in Brazil.

It was the first time she had ever felt like this about Pamela. She had always looked up to her mother, and as she grew older had admired the way she had brought her up single-handed. A courageous woman, she had thought, managing all these years without a man.

It had come as something of a shock when Ward told her that her father was alive. It had been the beginning of her disenchantment. And to discover now that her mother had encouraged various lovers, simply because her father had spent all his time working, was a disillusionment she felt unable to cope with at this precise moment.

She threw back the sheets and washed in the superb bathroom, wondering what she was supposed to wear that day. But when she opened the wardrobe and looked in the dressing-table drawers she discovered a whole new range of clothes. On her father's instructions someone must have gone shopping early. What a darling man he was!

Frilly undies and a pink cotton sundress fitted perfectly, and she literally danced her way into the dining room where she found Guy Pemberton reading a newspaper.

'Good morning, Father,' she trilled, 'and thank you for the lovely clothes. How did you know my size?'

He smiled tenderly. 'I didn't, Ward did. He sent them round earlier. Said it was his fault you'd had to leave your cases and this was the least he could do.'

Some of Verna's pleasure faded. 'He needn't have. I can't accept clothes from him. You will pay for them? I don't want to feel indebted.'

Guy frowned. 'Don't you and Ward get on? You surprise me. I thought you'd find him charming. If you insist, I'll pay, of course, but he won't like it. He's a stubborn character.'

'No more stubborn than me,' said Verna, her chin jutting. 'My mother brought me up to be independent. I don't want his charity.'

'I hardly think he would see it as that,' said her father. "Ward is very fair. If it was his fault your clothes were lost then he would consider it right and proper to replace them. Why can't you accept? What went on between you out there in the jungle?'

Verna shrugged. 'He lost his temper with me on several occasions. We're too much alike to get on.'

'And you maybe resented the fact that out there he was more knowledgeable than you? That you were not quite the tough little character Pamela brought up? The jungle is a wild, harsh place, Verna. You admitted that without Ward you wouldn't have survived. Don't think too badly of him. You'll probably find him a different person altogether now you're back in civilisation.'

'I was hoping I'd seen the last of him,' she said quietly.

'Why?' The word was sharp. 'Ward is my very dearest friend. He's round here a lot. If you two don't get on——' He did not finish, watching her closely, observing the faint flush beneath her skin.

Verna said hesitantly, but realising it had to be said, 'I think I love him, Father.'

He smiled, clearly relieved. 'So why are you worried? It would be perfect if you and he married.'

She shook her head. 'Ward doesn't love me. I won't lie and say that he didn't try anything—he did. But it meant nothing. I was just the only available woman. Let's leave it at that, shall we?'

He looked sad. 'I appreciate you telling me this, Verna. You didn't have to. But I can't help hoping that you're wrong. Ward's coming to dinner tonight. I shall watch you both closely and make up my own mind.'

Verna helped herself to rolls and butter and avoided looking at him. 'I wish you hadn't invited him—at least, not until I'd had time to look at my feelings.'

'I didn't know how you felt,' he said. 'And Ward comes quite often. He would think it strange if I didn't invite him, especially after all the trouble he's gone to to find you for me. I can't thank him enough, and he'll be welcome in my home at any time.'

He was hurt by her admission, but Verna did not regret telling him. There could be no secrets between them if they were to build up a deep and satisfying relationship. He was her father, after all, the only person she had in the world in whom she could confide. If he couldn't help her, no one could.

'I'll try to be nice to him,' she said, 'for your sake. But loving a man who doesn't love you in return isn't easy, and I'm not sure whether I'm capable of hiding my feelings. That's why I never wanted to see him again.'

Guy took her hands. 'Verna, my sweet, just be yourself. If you're radiant, Ward will think it's because of me, because we've found each other. Please don't ruin this happiest time of my life.'

'No, Father,' she said wryly. 'I'm being selfish,

and I'm sorry, and of course I won't spoil your pleasure.'

But for the rest of the day she could not help worrying. If she was truthful with herself she was longing to see Ward. A pulsing ache filled her limbs, nerves fluttered in her stomach, and she knew that she would have no peace until she saw him again.

She wondered what his attitude would be. Whether he would be completely offhand, which would be more than she could bear, or whether he would flirt outrageously, thus reducing her to a state of nervous trepidation. Or would he ignore her completely.

In the end she discovered that she was worrying needlessly. Ward arrived, dressed in a light lounge suit, looking even more handsome than she remembered. He greeted Guy warmly and herself as though she were an old—and platonic—friend.

She had dressed carefully in one of her new dresses, a peacock blue silk with thin straps and a full swirling skirt. She had brushed her hair until it shone like burnished gold, pinning it back behind her ears, in which she fastened two golden hoops. He had thought of everything, this man, even to a complete set of make-up and toilet accessories, and shoes to match all the various outfits.

Talk over dinner was inevitably about their adventures in the jungle, and Guy expressed extreme concern when Ward told him about Verna's attempt to gun down the jaguar.

'She had no thought for her own safety. It was me she was thinking of.' Ward smiled wryly. 'Thank God she missed, or we might have both been in danger. You know what a wounded cat can be like.'

'Give the girl credit,' said Guy. 'She could have

killed him outright. You wouldn't have scoffed at her fearlessness then.'

'I'm not scoffing,' said Ward with pretended indignation. 'I appreciate what she tried to do for me. I was pretty awful to her at times. It's a wonder she didn't let the jaguar make a meal of me and count her blessings that I was no longer around to aggravate her.'

'The thought did cross my mind,' said Verna pertly, 'except that I needed you to lead me out of the jungle.'

The bantering was goodnatured, and when they had finished and retired to the sitting room with their coffee, Verna felt that on the whole the evening had not gone off too badly. Certainly far better than she had expected.

But when her father suddenly declared that he was tired and intended going to bed, she felt quick alarm. Ward in her father's presence she could tolerate, but alone?

Her heartbeats accelerated alarmingly. 'I think I'll join you, Father,' she said, standing up. 'I've still not caught up on all the sleep I've lost. Do you mind, Ward? I'm sure you must be tired too.'

'Not in the least,' he said brightly, eyes alert.

He knew it was an excuse! And her father said, 'Nonsense, Verna. Stay and entertain my young friend. You can lie in in the morning. *Boa noite*, Verna. *Boa noite*, Ward.'

'Goodnight,' returned Ward. Verna merely smiled weakly and pecked his cheek, conscious that her father had done this deliberately.

'You've been on edge all evening,' said Ward once they were alone. 'Something tells me that you're not pleased to see me.'

'That's right,' she said tightly. 'I had enough of you in the jungle.' But despite her denial desire flared inside her and she turned away, wishing he weren't so aggressively attractive.

'You haven't thanked me for the new clothes,' he said, his fingers light upon her shoulders. 'Don't you think a kiss would be in order?'

'No, I don't,' she said crossly, quivering and longing to move into his arms. 'I didn't ask for them and I don't want them, and I told my father. He's going to reimburse you. No way am I going to be in your debt.'

'It was my fault you lost your others,' he said, eyes glinting darkly. 'And I didn't make a bad guess at the size either. You look enchanting.'

He toyed with the thin straps, sliding them from her shoulders, while Verna held her breath in trepidation. He lowered his head to trail kisses across her smooth, delicately perfumed skin. 'Mmm, you smell nice. Not that I had any complaints before. You assaulted my senses in the jungle—the same as you're doing now.'

Verna moved away sharply, unable to stand the sweet agony of his caress. 'Don't touch me, Ward! You can forget your jungle madness. This is civilisation. Please act like a civilised person.'

A grim smile appeared on his lips, not quite reaching his eyes. 'Little Miss Cool has returned, I see. Where's that hot passionate woman I discovered?'

'Left behind, I hope,' she snapped. 'Let's get one thing straight between us, Ward, since we shall apparently be seeing quite a lot of each other. I don't desire you. Whatever happened was a mistake, a moment of madness if you like. I'll be friends, because that's what my father wants, but as for anything else, you can forget it.'

Her words were harsh—they had to be. When he came near every fibre of her being responded to him, attack was her only form of defence.

'I don't believe you, Verna,' he said tightly. 'But if that's the way you want to play it, then carry on. You'll be the loser, not me.'

He turned and left and Verna's eyes filled with tears of self-pity and she wanted to call him back. She wanted him—on whatever terms. 'Ward,' she said softly, knowing that he could not hear. 'Ward, I love you—and you're right, I am the loser.'

This was the second time he had left her full of agonising despair, and she wondered whether she had the strength to carry on a charade of pretended indifference. For Guy's sake she must try, but only for him.

## CHAPTER TEN

AGAIN Verna slept in late and when she finally surfaced her father was keen to hear what had gone on between her and Ward.

'You left us alone deliberately,' she accused lightly. 'You weren't really tired, were you?'

His eyes twinkled. 'I could see you were eating your heart out for him, child. How did you get on?'

She said firmly, 'You're wasting your time trying to throw us together. I told him I was prepared to be his friend, for your sake, but nothing more.'

He shook his head sadly. 'You're a fool, Verna. I'm quite sure he has more than a passing interest in you. I watched you both carefully last night and I know him well, don't forget. He's had girls in plenty, I won't dispute that, but he's never quite been the same with them as he is with you.'

'Lord help them, then,' said Verna irreverently.

'No, you don't know what I mean. Ward usually flirts outrageously, but he treated you with respect, as though you were someone very special. He teased you, I admit, but it was all in the nicest possible way. Why don't you let him see how you feel?'

She hung her head. 'I tried it once,' she said quietly. 'I virtually offered myself to him—and do you know what he did? He rejected me. He walked out and left me. I've never been so humilated in all my life!'

'Perhaps that wasn't what he wanted,' said the

old man wisely. 'Maybe he wants to hear that you love him by word, not deed.'

'And risk him laughing at me?' cried Verna. 'No, thank you very much! I know exactly how Ward Levitt feels about me. I amuse him. He likes to get beneath my skin, he likes to see me in a temper, and then he laughs. I hate him!'

Guy Pemberton shook his head. 'I understand, but I also know that I lost my wife through my own stupidity. Don't lose Ward the same way.'

'I haven't got him,' Verna flashed. 'Let's talk about something else. He leaves a nasty taste in my mouth.'

He shrugged and looked sad. 'As you wish. I think I ought to warn you, though, he's taking you to Belém this afternoon.'

Her eyes flew wide and she began to protest, but he silenced her with a lift of his hand. 'I'm not fit enough to take you myself, dearest Verna, much as I'd like to.'

'So you nominated Ward in your place? Thanks a lot, that's just what I need!'

Guy was upset, and Verna felt quick regret that she was causing him so much unhappiness. 'I could have gone alone,' she told him.

'It's not the same; he'll know exactly where to take you.'

'Of course.' She smiled and gave him a quick hug. 'I'm an ungrateful wretch, and I'm sorry. I'll be nice to Ward this afternoon, I really will.'

But later, as she was getting ready for her outing, she could not help but feel irritated that the two men had planned this in secret. Why hadn't she been asked? Because they knew she would refuse?

She was amazed that Ward had agreed, knowing the way she felt about him. Was he being nice to her for Guy's sake, or, an unlikely thought, was it because he really did care about her, as her father had suggested?

It would be wonderful if he did, it would be the culmination of her dreams, but somehow she could not see it. Ward was very fond of her father and whatever he was doing was for this older man.

He arrived shortly after lunch, looking cool and devastating in a white short-sleeved shirt and cream pants. Simply looking at him tore her in two, and after greeting him she turned away, unable to bear the sweet torment, afraid her love might reveal itself in her eyes.

Her own dress was a crisp yellow cotton, loose and comfortable, with matching low-heeled sandals. She had clipped her hair up on top and wore a white straw hat with tiny yellow flowers decorating the brim.

The air-conditioning in the house had kept it delightfully cool, but once outside the thick humid heat caught in her throat. She had forgotten how hot Brazil was.

At first she had wondered whether the hat wasn't a bit too dressy for the occasion, but now she was glad of its protection against the merciless rays of the sun. She slid on a pair of dark glasses which Ward had also thoughtfully provided, and immediately relaxed. Behind them she could hide from him. They were an admirable defence.

His car was cool, but once they had parked and began their tour of the city Verna felt perspiration trickle down her spine and the sickly cloying heat reminded her of the jungle.

Ward had not spoken much and she began to feel irritated, and the heat did not help. 'If you're here from a sense of duty, you needn't have bothered,' she said tetchily.

'And what makes you think that?' He stopped walking, right there in the middle of the pavement, and looked down at her. His eyes too were hidden behind sunglasses, but the grimness of his lips told her that he was angry.

'I thought you were supposed to be showing me Belém? You've told me nothing about it yet. All we've done is walk and walk. I haven't a clue what I'm looking at.'

'You don't exactly strike me as being in a very receptive frame of mind.' He caught her arm and pulled her to one side as a crowd of youths came running past.

'Because I didn't want to come with you,' she defended. 'You had no right arranging things behind my back!'

'It was your father's suggestion,' he said. 'Naturally I thought he'd consulted you. I was surprised, admittedly, knowing how you feel about me.'

'But you never thought of refusing?'

'I'd do anything for Guy,' he said simply.

'Even at the cost of your own happiness?'

His brows rose caustically. 'That would depend. Surprising as it may seem, I was quite looking forward to today. A pity you're ruining it by acting like a spoilt child.'

'No, I am not!' she replied indignantly. 'You're the one who's in a mood.'

Ward heaved a sigh but said nothing, his lips tightening as he took her arm and led her firmly forward. They walked beside the river through a busy fish market. The stalls were palm-thatched and sold all sorts of exotic fish, including six-foot-long sharks hanging by their tails and smelling atrocious.

In the bird market there were innumerable varieties on sale, all sitting in small bamboo cages and clamouring for attention. There were tiny songbirds, parrots and parakeets, as well as live chickens and ducks in wicker baskets.

There were even small monkeys prancing on the ends of chains, and they looked so sweet Verna would have dearly loved one, though she realised the impracticality of keeping such a pet and kept her thoughts to herself.

Further on was the meat market, and she was disgusted to see the fly-covered chunks of meat, and overhead great black vultures eyeing the food hungrily, occasionally flying down to grab a piece while the owner was not looking.

It revolted her and she said, 'Let's go, I've seen enough.'

They wandered along cobbled streets admiring the romantic architecture and houses decorated with Romeo and Juliet balconies. They strolled past picturesque fishing boats in a tiny harbour, the fishermen waving to them cheerfully.

There was a mixture of old and new in Belém. Tall concrete tower blocks stood side by side with frivolously spired churches.

They spent an hour in the museum looking at a collection of native tools, arrows, armour and Indian fetishes, all reminding Verna of the time they had spent amongst the Indian tribes. Outside the museum was a zoo with tapirs and snakes, crocodiles, monkeys and tropical birds.

'It's a shame for them to be shut up here,' she protested. 'Why don't they let them go free?'

'You have zoos in England,' said Ward. 'What's the difference?'

'I don't believe in penning up wild animals,' she

answered firmly. She had always felt strongly about this, but even more so since she had actually seen the animals living in the wild.

'These probably don't know any other way of life.' He took her arm and led her away. 'I could do with a drink. How about you?'

They enjoyed ice-cold beer in a charming restaurant, but Verna did not feel at ease. Their conversation was polite, stilted, like two strangers meeting for the first time, and she was relieved when Ward suggested they make their way home.

Verna knew she had no one to blame but herself. She had insisted that their relationship be nothing but friendly—and that only for the sake of her father.

But it hurt. It hurt like hell. She craved physical contact. She desperately longed for him to show some sign of affection, of desiring her, even though she knew that that was all it would be—desire!

Consequently by the time they arrived back at her father's house she was petulant and irritable and longing for the solace of her own room to give way to her soul-destroying tears.

It came as a shock when her father said she had a visitor. 'Who is it?' she laughed. 'I don't know anyone in Brazil.'

'Find out for yourself,' he smiled mysteriously.

Verna walked into the sitting room, saw the tall familiar figure, and flung herself into his arms. 'David! Oh, David!'

'Hey, what a welcome!' he grinned. 'I certainly didn't expect that!'

She had never been demonstrative where David was concerned. They were good friends, that was all—very good friends. But the relief of seeing someone she knew, someone she could depend upon and trust without any complications in their relationship, and at a time when she was feeling raw and hurt by Ward's treatment, was almost more than she could stand.

She clung to his hands, pulling him down on the settee beside her, her eyes searching his face. 'What are you doing here? Gosh, I'm so surprised! You could have knocked me down with a feather!'

'You promised to phone,' he said with mock severity. 'At least, you promised to phone Jenny the moment you arrived, and she's been going out of her mind with worry. In the end I agreed to come over and find out what had happened. I think she thought your Mr Levitt had absconded with you, that the story about your father had all been a con.'

Verna glanced at Guy Pemberton and smiled fondly. 'As you can see, he's very much a real figure. I expect he's told you what happened? What an experience! I never want to go through that again. Though Ward was a——'

Looking round, she discovered he had disappeared. She felt absurdly disappointed. Why hadn't he waited to be introduced? She had told him about David, wasn't he interested in meeting an old friend?

'He's gone,' she said unnecessarily, not realising her chagrin was mirrored on her face. 'Never mind, you'll meet him some other time. Are you staying long?'

David looked at her father. 'It all depends on how long Guy will put up with me.'

Her father smiled. 'As long as you like, young man. Any friend of Verna's is welcome here. It's almost time for dinner, Verna. Go and get ready, then you can spend all evening talking to David.'

She went to her room, a little bemused by this turn of events, and puzzled why Ward had departed so abruptly. But she was not downhearted for long. David had brought a breath of England with him, and she was longing for news of Jenny and all her old friends.

Dinner was a jolly meal. Verna felt almost her old self, able to forget Ward in David's pleasant company. He was so natural that she felt relaxed and happy and treated him with far more affection than she had ever previously shown.

He noticed it too, and when they finally retired he kissed her goodnight with considerably more feeling than on previous occasions. And Verna wondered what had come over him.

The next day Verna took David out and showed him the town, and they spent a lot of time laughing and having fun, and she realised exactly how much she had missed London, and her friends, and her happy organised life.

She felt homesick, and had it not been for her father, who was so genuinely delighted to have her here, and who would be heartbroken if she left, she would have seriously considered returning to London with David.

David was different, though, more possessive in his attitude. In the past he had treated her more as a sister, but now there was a difference in their relationship. Several times she caught him looking at her with a singularly lovesick expression, and she could hardly perceive that this was the same David.

Constantly he slipped his arm about her waist or held her hand when they were out walking. His kisses were tentative, however, as if he was unsure of his reception, and because she felt sorry for him Verna tried to show a little more enthusiasm. At least he was helping her forget Ward.

The days passed quickly. There seemed so much to do and David was absorbed with ideas for new paintings, taking his sketch pad with him wherever they went, sometimes sitting painting while Verna watched or wandered away on her own.

Gradually she had become accustomed to the thick heat. She no longer felt quite so enervated, and then, of course, when they returned home the house was always delightfully cool.

Her father approved of her friendship with David—or at least he seemed to. He never spoke of Ward, except to say occasionally that it was unusual for him not to have come round, or at least phoned to see how he was keeping.

'He knows you have me to look after you now,' smiled Verna tenderly. 'Dear Father! I do wish I'd known you when I was a child.'

His smile was sad. 'I missed the best years of your life. My only fear now is that you'll grow restless and decide to return to England.'

'I do miss it,' she admitted. 'Don't you ever fancy going back there?'

He shook his head firmly. 'No, child. I intend to spend the rest of my days here. This is my home now.'

'And mine,' she said impulsively. 'I won't leave you, Father—not ever.'

'You're a good girl,' he said. 'I shall never be out of Ward's debt.' He seemed about to say something else, then changed his mind.

'How long have you known David?' he asked instead. 'He seems a fine man. He's very fond of you.'

'Years,' said Verna airily. 'We're just good

friends, nothing more. He's the only man I've ever felt completely at ease with.'

'Mmm.' Guy looked thoughtful. 'Speaking as an observer I would say David wants more than just friendship. I hope you're not going to hurt him—he's far too decent.'

Verna nodded. 'To be quite frank, Father, he does seem different out here. I expect it's because I'm the only person he knows. He doesn't mean anything by it.'

Guy said no more, but he did not look entirely convinced, and Verna wondered whether she ought to have a word with David. If he really was getting ideas about her, it would be best to stop it now before he got too involved.

It had seemed a good idea in the beginning to encourage him, he helped her forget Ward, but if he did think himself in love with her, she was not doing him the least bit of good by pretending to be fonder of him than she really was. She knew only too well what it was like to love and not be loved in return.

As usual, her father returned shortly after dinner, leaving her and David in the sitting room. Normally they played records and chatted constantly about anything and everything, but tonight he looked nervous, unable to settle, drinking rather more of Guy's whisky than was his habit.

Verna found it difficult to know where to start. Had they been sitting quietly together there would have been no problem; she could have broached the subject easily. But David was restless, as though he too had something on his mind and was not quite sure how to tackle it.

She stood up and went across to him, taking the glass carefully from his hand and placing it on a nearby table. 'David,' she said, 'there's something we must discuss,' and to lessen the blow she reached up and kissed him gently on the lips.

His eyes lightened fractionally. 'So you feel it too? I wondered. Oh, Verna, I'm so glad!' and before she had time to realise what was happening he had pulled her roughly into his arms and began showering her with hot passionate kisses.

When she did not respond he held her away from him a fraction. 'My darling! I've frightened you? I'm so sorry, but I've held back for so long. I was afraid you didn't feel the same—you've always been so cool and remote. But now I know that you do I can't wait. Please, Verna, please say you'll marry me!'

It was all going dreadfully wrong. Verna closed her eyes, feeling herself sway weakly against him. Why hadn't she seen what was happening?

She, who thought she knew all about men, had never dreamt for one moment that David, her dear dependable David, entertained such hopes. Had he loved her all these years? Had he been as stricken when she showed no signs of returning his love as she was about Ward?

She ought to have known when he came over here. His tale about Jenny being worried was all an excuse. No man would come all these miles unless the girl in question meant something to him. What an idiot she was! And how was she going to get out of it without hurting him terribly?

It seemed an age that she stood there, although it could have been no more than a few seconds. Her eyes fluttered open again. 'David,' she said plaintively. 'Oh, David, what can I say?'

Over his shoulder she caught a movement in the mirror. Ward's eyes met her own and she was appalled at the agony in their depths.

She whirled. 'Ward! I didn't know you were here. Father never said he expected you.'

His face was shuttered now, blank, completely devoid of all expression. 'Quite obviously,' he said coldly, and to David, 'Congratulations. You're a very lucky man.' Then he turned on his heel and left.

'Wait!' cried Verna. 'You don't understand. Please, Ward, don't go!'

But it was too late. The front door closed with a decisive click. Ward had walked out of her life—for ever!

She felt very close to tears and groped wildly for a chair. Her legs were strangely weak and her face had drained of all colour, leaving it ashen, her eyes two green pools of despair.

David sat her down and looked at her sorrowfully. 'Seems like I jumped the gun. You were going to tell me about Ward, weren't you? That you loved him and not me? I apologise if I've messed things up for you. Shall I go after him? I can explain, I——'

'No!' Verna shook her head emphatically. 'Leave it, David. Ward doesn't love me, he never has.'

'But you love him?'

She nodded. 'I'm sorry, I never knew you felt this way—not until my father mentioned it. I've been a blind fool, and if I've caused you to be unhappy, I apologise. I know being sorry won't help, but I couldn't marry you, David, not feeling the way I do about Ward. It wouldn't be fair. I'm very fond of you and I'd like to think we can always be friends—if that's not too much to ask?'

'I think it would be best if I went back to England.' His face was tight and hurt, and she could not blame him. 'I'll probably be gone when you get up in the morning. Goodbye, Verna. Good luck.'

He went then, but it was a long time before Verna could drag herself up. What a mess she had made of her life—David's too. That was the worst part about it. She would never forgive herself for not realising that he had feelings too, that all these years he had been biding his time, waiting for the right moment.

And when he had thought he had her on his side, she had destroyed him, just as Ward was destroying her.

It was a pity she could not get out of it so easily and go back to England herself. But she had promised her father and no way would she fail him. He at least loved and needed her, and she would devote herself to him for his remaining years.

She would give no thought to herself and maybe in time she would learn to regard Ward as a friend. Perhaps if she tried hard enough she could push her love right out of her mind, forget it had ever existed.

With these noble thoughts she went to bed, but lay for long hours staring into the darkness. She would have given anything for Ward not to have witnessed that scene tonight.

The next morning her father told her that David had been called unexpectedly back to England. 'I was surprised, I must admit. But it could be for the best. I think I'll invite Ward over to dinner tonight. I don't want you feeling lonely.'

'No, don't do that,' said Verna quickly, and because she knew she was sounding irrational. 'I'd like to spend some time with you. I've neglected you shamefully while David's been here.'

'Ward's no intruder,' he said warmly. 'He's almost one of the family.' He frowned suddenly. 'Actually he was supposed to come last night for an after-dinner drink, but I suppose something cropped up.'

Verna said nothing. 'I'll leave it to you, Father. It's your house.'

He looked cross for a second. 'Yours too now, my child, and don't you forget it.'

They spent the rest of the day carefully avoiding mentioning Ward's name, but Verna knew that her father had phoned him. What she did not know was whether he had accepted the invitation.

By dinner she felt a nervous wreck and spent an age applying make-up in an endeavour to disguise her shadowed eyes. If Ward did come she did not want him to know that she was anything other than deliriously happy.

There were three places set in the dining room. She kissed her father's cheek dutifully when she entered. 'Ward is coming, then?'

Guy nodded and smiled. 'You look very nice this evening. White suits you, with that glorious tan. Ward will be flattered you've taken so much trouble over your appearance.'

She doubted it, but said nothing. 'Is he late, or am I early?'

He looked at his watch. 'He'll be here any moment now,' and as if on cue they heard the sound of his car. Verna felt apprehensive, her fingers fluttering over her hair, glancing selfconsciously into the mirror.

Her reflection was one of complete confidence, poised and cool, with none of her inner torment showing. She turned as the door opened, smiled politely, and said, 'Good evening, Ward. It's nice to see you again.'

'Is it?' he snarled.

He wore a navy velvet dinner jacket and a pale blue silk shirt, and she felt devastated by the mere sight of him. Her fingers trembled and she hid them behind her back. 'Father and I were wondering why we haven't seen so much of you lately.'

'That's right,' added Guy. 'Where have you been hiding yourself? Pressure of work?'

'You could say that.' Ward's eyes flashed, as deep blue as his jacket. 'After a wasted week there was plenty to do.'

A wasted week! Was that what he thought? Verna cringed inwardly, but was determined not to spoil the evening for her father. 'I'm sorry if it was my fault,' she said sweetly.

He looked at her angrily. 'It was mine as much as yours. I should have had the plane checked more thoroughly. Please don't feel guilty on my behalf.'

'I think we ought to eat,' said her father, in an endeavour to ease the tension. 'Carolina won't be pleased if we keep dinner waiting.'

Ward looked at the table, observing with narrowed eyes the three place settings. 'Where's your fiancé?' he enquired suddenly of Verna. 'Deserted you so soon?'

'What are you talking about?' asked Guy sharply. 'David has returned to England, but——'

'You didn't know he asked your daughter to marry him?' Ward's eyes were alight with malicious intent. 'Oh, yes, I walked in on the tender scene last night. Why didn't you tell your father, Verna? Were you waiting for the right moment? Afraid he might not approve of you marrying a struggling artist?'

'What is this?' Guy Pemberton looked completely bemused. 'Verna?'

She lifted her chin stubbornly. 'It's true—David did ask me to marry him. I'm sorry I didn't tell you.'

Guy frowned and looked angry, and Verna had never seen him like this before.

At that moment, to her relief, Carolina swept in with their first course—tiny stuffed crab shells which Verna knew were delicious, but which tasted like sawdust tonight. She pushed hers away hardly touched and sat and watched as Ward finished his with obvious relish.

Her father filled her wine glass, eyeing her sharply all the time. She drank it quickly and asked for more. Drowning her sorrows seemed the only solution.

No more was said about David. Her father and Ward talked about work and Verna continued to drink. She toyed with her charcoal-grilled steak, cutting it into little pieces and sliding them round her plate, but quite unable to face the thought of eating.

Now and then she caught her father watching her, but she studiously pretended not to notice. Ward ignored her altogether, not even once glancing in her direction, enjoying the excellent meal and conversing with Guy as though they were the only two in the room.

She wondered whether they would notice if she slipped away.

And then suddenly their meal was over and her father led her into the sitting room, holding her arm firmly so that there was no chance of escape.

Would he follow his normal practice and go to bed early? She hoped not. She did not feel she could face up to Ward in the aggressive mood he was in.

It was soul-destroying, being forced into the company of this man whom she loved dearly, and she found she was shivering so violently that her coffee cup rattled in its saucer.

Ward smiled tightly and took it from her. Her

stomach did an about-turn at his nearness and she carefully kept her eyes lowered. 'What a state he's got you into,' he muttered savagely. 'Sit down before you fall down!'

She obeyed, her movements stiff and automatic. If you only knew, she thought. Don't you know that it's you who's breaking my heart?

Somehow she managed to finish her coffee and her father said sharply, 'I think you'd better fetch her another one, Ward. She's drunk far too much wine. I can't think what's got into her.'

'She's missing the boy-friend, I expect,' he sneered, deliberately tossing her a condemning glance as he left the room.

The moment the door closed her father said, 'Now, Verna, suppose you tell me what this is all about? Did David ask you to marry him?'

She nodded, unable to hold his gaze.

'What did I tell you?' he savaged. 'Did you accept?'

She took a deep breath and shook her head.

'Then why the hell didn't you tell us?' A look of relief crossed his face. 'Why did you let both Ward and me assume that you'd agreed to become his wife?'

'Because it's better this way,' she said, wringing her hands, and imploring him to understand.

'For whom?' he grated. 'You—or Ward? So far as I can see you're both desperately unhappy. I've never known Ward in such a foul mood. He looks as though he positively hates you!'

'He does,' she snapped.

'Nonsense! You're a pair of idiots, and if you don't both come to your senses I shall do something about it myself, much as I hate interfering.'

'Father! You wouldn't?' Verna was appalled. 'If you tell Ward I love him I'll never forgive you, not as long as I live. I shall go back to England and ——'

'And what?'

The soft words caused her to jerk sharply round. Ward stood in the doorway, her cup of coffee in one hand, his other on the handle, an absurd mixture of hope and disbelief on his face.

Verna crumpled and dissolved into tears, and tried to dash from the room, totally embarrassed. 'It's your fault, Father,' she sobbed.

Ward caught her arm as she attempted to brush past, the coffee cup went flying, and she was imprisoned against the hard strength of him.

His mouth was fierce and urgent against her own, his self-control snapping as he hungrily demanded her submission. Verna gave up and clung to him, still sobbing, unable to comprehend, but responding gladly, pressing her body achingly against his, aware of his throbbing passion.

Neither of them noticed Guy slip quietly from the room, a look of complete approval on his face. And when Ward carried her across to the settee, laying her down gently before covering her body with his own, Verna had no thought of resisting.

At length, their initial hunger assuaged, Ward eased himself away. 'Why didn't you let me know you loved me, you little fool?' He sounded angry. 'And why did you let me think you'd accepted your artist friend's proposal?'

She looked apologetic. 'I thought it was for the best.'

'You thought!' he rasped. 'Don't you care what I think? Doesn't it matter that I've been going half out of my mind yearning for you, that it's been killing me keeping away from this place? I've seen you with David. I've seen the fun you've had together. Verna, you've almost driven me out of my mind!'

'I didn't know,' she said softly, but there was a song in her heart.

'I love you, Verna,' he said harshly. 'I love you, love you, love you, and don't you ever forget it. You're mine, and no other man shall have you.'

He was positively vicious in his declaration and Verna pulled him close, kissing him freely, exulting in his final admission of love.

'You don't know how I've longed to hear you say that!' Her face was pale and she trembled in his arms. 'I thought that—you just wanted my body. I had no idea that you——'

He silenced her with another kiss, gently this time, experiencing the softness of her mouth, gazing deeply into her eyes which were full of love and wonder—and agonising desire.

'You began to get under my skin not long after we landed in the jungle,' he told her. 'I began to realise what a wonderful woman you were, not at all like the person I'd first met. You were too much in command then, I didn't like you at all. I like my women soft and sensitive, and totally responsive to a man.'

Verna moved her body sensually against him. 'I only have to look at you for my body to leap into flames. You're so dominantly male, exactly the type my mother warned me against. How I love you!'

He smiled triumphantly. 'Am I glad you don't always take her advice! Will you marry me, sweetest? Or is it too much for you to get two proposals in two days?'

She nibbled his ear and whispered wickedly, 'It's very flattering.'

He said thickly, 'I felt like killing both you and

David last night. Quite how I managed to get out of the house without doing it I'll never know.'

'Are you glad now?' she twinkled impishly.

He groaned and possessed her mouth, and she felt the throb of his heart wild and strong, and her love welled and she marvelled that anyone could be so happy as she was right at this moment.

'You once said you valued your freedom too much to get married?' she probed gently.

'I did,' said Ward. 'But that was before I met you. Somehow you managed to get through my thick skin. Quite how you did it I'll never know. Plenty have tried and not succeeded.'

'I'm jealous,' she said loudly. 'I want to be the only woman in your life, the only woman you've ever made love to, the only woman——'

'How about David?' he asked grimly.

'What about David? He's never meant anything to me. Our relationship was purely platonic.'

'That's not what you told me.' His face was angry now and he moved away from the settee, standing over her, as aloof as he had ever been.

She shivered, suddenly cold. 'Ward?' She tried to touch him, but he backed away. 'You must be mistaken. There's never been anything between David and me.'

'He painted you in the nude,' he accused.

'That was art,' she cried. 'He never touched me—he's not like that.'

'And that day in the jungle when you told me he was different. You virtually set him up on a pedestal, apart from all men. What the hell did you expect me to believe?'

Verna laughed. 'Oh, Ward! He *was* different. That was the beauty of David. He never tried anything. When he said he loved me last night I was flabbergasted. Apparently he'd felt like it all these years, but never said anything, because he was afraid. It was he who set me up on a pedestal. I was untouchable. Obviously I reacted too strongly when he came here. I was so pleased to see a friendly face that I overdid it and he thought he'd take a chance and pop the question.'

'Are you sure?' He still looked unconvinced, his eyes cold and hard, his mouth set.

'Of course I'm sure, Ward.' In desperation she reached out. 'You're the only one I've ever loved or ever wanted, and if you reject me now I shall do what you wanted to do last night—and kill myself.'

With a cry he crushed her to him. 'Verna, my darling Verna! I believe you. I hated David once, now I'm sorry for him. All I can say is that he's a fool for not voicing his feelings earlier. Would you have married him if he'd asked you before you met me?'

She shook her head. 'He wasn't for me. I think there's only one man for each woman in this whole wide world, and when you meet him you know, and unless you're very foolish you don't let him go.'

'You almost lost me,' he said tenderly.

'I don't know,' she replied. 'I think in the end I'd have swallowed my pride and come to you. My father had already told me you loved me. He could see it where I couldn't.'

He nodded. 'He's an astute man. I shall enjoy having him as a father-in-law. Not that it will be much different. I never knew my own parents. Guy's always treated me like a son. I think we shall make one very happy family.'

'Let's tell him,' said Verna, bubbling over with her love for this man.

Ward smiled. 'I should be surprised if he doesn't

already know. In fact I suspect he made up his mind long before we did ourselves, and he'd have been acutely unhappy if we'd disappointed him.'

'I'm glad we didn't,' she said softly.

'So am I,' he said, as he kissed her again. 'So am I.'

*Harlequin*® **Plus**

## THE COLORFUL PARAKEET

One of the great delights of living in such tropical countries as Brazil is the abundance of the unusual indigenous wildlife. One common sight (and sound) of the tropics is the parakeet, screeching and squawking high in a palm tree. And while parakeets might often sound as if they are quarreling, their racket is most likely playful rather than serious. For parakeets are a kind of parrot renowned for their affection for each other.

Close relatives of the parakeet include budgerigars or "budgies," as well as the larger macaws and cockatoos. These highly intelligent and colorful birds are a joy to see (and hear) in the wild. But as well, for thousands of years, the different species of parrots have made amusing and affectionate pets. Alexander the Great is said to have brought one from India as a gift for his teacher, Aristotle; a Roman expedition sent to find the source of the Nile returned with African parrots for the Emperor Nero.

Parakeets are easy to take care of in the home, although their beaks, designed by nature for crushing seeds, can be dangerous. The South African parakeet can inflict a nasty bite; and its big cousin the macaw can take off a finger!

But the most astonishing characteristic of these birds is their ability to imitate a wide range of sounds, including human speech. It takes a great deal of patience to teach them because they learn by constant repetition, and then only if they know and trust their human companion. The result, however, is worth it!